THE BIG NAP

NURSERY CRIMES

"A humorous tale . . . . Juliet's voice is strong and appealing, and the Hollywood satire is dead on."   —*Publishers Weekly*

"Funny, clever, touching, original, wacky, and wildly successful."   —Carolyn G. Hart

"A delightful debut filled with quirky, engaging characters, sharp wit, and vivid prose. I predict a successful future for this unique, highly likable sleuth."

                              —Judith Kelman, author of *After the Fall*

continued on next page . . .

"Told with warmth and wicked humor, *Nursery Crimes* is a rollicking first mystery that will leave you clamoring for more. Ruby's adorable and Juliet is the sort of outspoken and funny woman we'd all like as a best friend."

—*Romantic Times*

"[Waldman] derives humorous mileage from Juliet's 'epicurean' cravings, wardrobe dilemmas, night-owl husband, and obvious delight in adventure."   —*Library Journal*

"Unique . . . will intrigue anyone who values a good mystery novel."   —*The Tribune-Review Pittsburgh*

"[Waldman is] a welcome voice . . . well-written . . . this charming young family has a real-life feel to it."

—*Contra Costa Times*

THE BIG NAP

Ayelet Waldman

BERKLEY PRIME CRIME, NEW YORK

This is a work of fiction. Names, characters, places, and incidents either are the product of the author's imagination or are used fictitiously, and any resemblance to actual persons, living or dead, business establishments, events, or locales is entirely coincidental.

THE BIG NAP

A Berkley Prime Crime Book / published by arrangement with the author

PRINTING HISTORY
Berkley Prime Crime hardcover edition / June 2001
Berkley Prime Crime mass-market edition / July 2002

Copyright © 2001 by Ayelet Waldman.
Cover art by Lisa Desimini.

Visit our website at
www.penguinputnam.com

ISBN: 0-425-18452-8

Berkley Prime Crime Books are published
by The Berkley Publishing Group,
a division of Penguin Putnam Inc.,
375 Hudson Street, New York, New York 10014.
The name BERKLEY PRIME CRIME and the BERKLEY PRIME
CRIME design are trademarks belonging to Penguin Putnam Inc.

PRINTED IN THE UNITED STATES OF AMERICA

10 9 8 7 6 5 4 3

For Michael, Sophie, and Zeke

Author's Note

For helping me to understand the Hasidic community I thank Karen Zivan, Alex Novack, and the incomparable Esther Strauss. All mistakes are most definitely my own. For medical information I thank Dr. Dean Schillinger. I am eternally grateful to Mary Evans and to my husband, Michael Chabon, without whom nothing is possible.

One

I probably wasn't the first woman who had ever opened the door to the Fed Ex man wearing nothing from the waist up except for a bra. Odds are I was not even the first to do it in a *nursing* bra. But I'm willing to bet that no woman in a nursing bra had ever before greeted our apple-cheeked Fed Ex man with her flaps unsnapped and gaping wide-open. You could see that in his face.

I thought about being embarrassed, but decided that since I'd been too tired to notice that I wasn't dressed, I was definitely too tired to care. "You have to air-dry them," I explained. "Or they can crack."

"That has to hurt," he said.

I signed for the package, which turned out to be yet another sterling silver rattle from Tiffany (that made seven), closed the door, and dragged myself up the stairs to the second-floor, duplex apartment where I lived with my husband, Peter, my three-year-old daughter, Ruby, and the mutant vampire to whom I'd given birth four months before.

"Yes, yes, yes. I know," I sang in a mock cheerful voice as I scooped my screaming baby out of his bassinet. "Finished your six-minute nap, have you? That's all the sleep you'll be needing this week, isn't it? Hmm?"

Isaac eyed my conveniently exposed nipple and increased the pitch of his wail. I settled my bulk into the aggressively ugly glider rocker that had taken pride of place in our living room and lifted him to my breast. He began suckling as though he'd just gotten home from vacation in Biafra. It had been all of half an hour since he'd eaten. I leaned back in the chair, ran my tongue over my unbrushed teeth, and looked up at the clock on the mantelpiece. Noon. And I'd been awake for eight hours. Actually, it's hardly fair to say that I woke up at 4:00 A.M. That was just when I'd finally abandoned the pretense that night was a time when we, like the rest of the world, slept. Isaac Applebaum Wyeth never slept. Never. Like really never. It was my firm belief that in the four months since his birth the kid hadn't closed his eyes for longer than twenty minutes at a stretch. Okay, that's not fair. There was that one time when he slept for three hours straight. But since I was at the doctor's office having a wound check (bullet and cesarean, but that's another story altogether) at the time of this miracle, I had only Isaac's father's word that it had actually occurred. And I had my doubts.

Sitting there, nursing Isaac, I entertained myself by imagining what I would be doing if I were still a federal public defender and not a bedraggled stay-at-home mom. First of all, by this hour of the day I'd have already finished three or four bail hearings. I might be on the way to the Metropolitan Detention Center, hoping my smack-addict clients were straight enough to have a conversation about their plea agreements. Or, I might be in trial, striding around the courtroom, tearing into a quivering FBI agent and exposing his testimony for the web of lies that it was. All right, all right. Maybe not. Maybe I'd be watching my client self-destruct on the stand while he explained that the reason he was covered in red paint and holding the sack of the bank's money complete with the exploding dye pack was because his friend borrowed his clothes and car and did the robbery and then mysteriously gave him the bag. And no, he doesn't remember his friend's name.

But I wasn't a public defender anymore. I wasn't even a lawyer. I was just an overtired, underdressed mother. I'd quit the job I'd loved so much when Ruby was a baby. This decision shocked the hell out of everyone who knew me. It certainly hadn't been part of the plan I'd set out for myself when I walked down the aisle at Harvard Law School with the big diploma emblazoned with the words "Juliet Applebaum, *Juris Doctorat*." I'd left Cambridge brimming over with ambition and student loans and began my career as a corporate lawyer, a job I hated but with a salary I really needed.

Then, one day, I got into an argument with the clerk in my local video store that changed my life. Never, when I started dating the slightly geeky, gray-eyed slacker who gave me such a hard time when I rented *Pretty Woman*, did I imagine that he'd pay off my student loans with the proceeds of a movie called *Flesh Eaters* and move me out to Los Angeles.

My husband Peter's success had given me the freedom I needed to have the career I really wanted, as a criminal defense lawyer. Our decision to start a family had derailed me completely. I know lots of women manage to be full-time mothers and productive members of the work force at the same time, but, much to my surprise, I wasn't one of them. When I tried to do both I succeeded only in being incompetent at work and short-tempered at home. At some point I realized that it would be better for my daughter to have me around, and if I was bored out of my skull, so be it.

Isaac must have gotten sick of listening to me yawn, because he popped off my breast, let loose a massive belch, and graced me with a huge smile. He was, like his sister before him, bald but for a fringe of hair around the sides of his lumpy skull. He had a little hooked nose and a perennially worried expression that made him look, for all the world, like a beleaguered Jewish accountant and inspired his father to christen him with the nickname Murray Kleinfeld, CPA.

I kissed him a few times under his chins and hoisted myself up out of the chair.

"Ready to face the day?" I wasn't sure who I was asking—my four-month-old son or myself.

Only a mother of an infant knows that it is in fact possible to take a shower, wash your hair, and shave your legs, all within a single verse of "Old MacDonald Had a Farm." The trick is finishing the E-I E-I O's with your toothbrush in your mouth.

Balancing Isaac on my hip, I gazed at my reflection critically. Washed and artfully ruffled, my cropped red hair looked pretty good, as long as you weren't looking too intently at the roots. My face had lost some of that pregnancy bloat, although sometimes it did seem as though Isaac and I were competing to see who could accumulate the most chins. My eyes still shone bright green and I decided to do my best to emphasize the only feature not affected by my rather astonishing weight gain. I applied a little mascara.

All in all, if I was careful not to glance below my neck, I wasn't too hideous.

"Isn't your mama gorgeous?" I asked the baby. He gave me a Bronx cheer.

I rubbed some lipstick off my teeth.

"Let's get dressed."

A mere half-hour later, a record for the newly enlarged Wyeth-Applebaum household, Isaac and I were in the car on our way to pick up Ruby at preschool. He was, as usual, screaming, and I was, as usual, singing hysterically along with the Raffi tape that played on a continuous loop in my Volvo station wagon.

One really has to wonder how children make it to the age of ten without being pitched headfirst out a car window.

Two

ON the way home, my children thoughtfully contrived to keep me from falling asleep at the wheel—not an easy task given that I'd been averaging more or less eleven minutes of sleep a night—by regaling me, at top volume with (in one ear) a long, involved story about Sneakers the rat and how he had escaped from his cage, and (in the other) the usual hysterical weeping.

As we pulled into our driveway, Ruby said, "Mama, can we go to the park? Please oh please oh please oh please."

It was only because I was momentarily distracted by thoughts of the proper diagnosis of sleep-deprivation psychosis that I forgot that I'd been looking forward to turning on *Sesame Street* and enjoying an hour or so of TV-induced stupor (mine rather than theirs).

"Okay, honey," I said. Oh well, there was always the possibility that Isaac would fall asleep on the way there. I bundled the two of them into their double stroller and set off for a walk to the playground.

Our neighborhood, Hancock Park, is one of the oldest in Los Angeles, dating all the way back to the 1920s. It's full of big old houses, most of them stuccoed Spanish-style numbers with the occasional elaborate English Tudor thrown in for variety. The broad tree-lined avenues arc in gentle, carefully planned curves. While the addresses might have hinted at a certain long-ago grandeur, the neighborhood's proximity to downtown L.A. and a number of less savory neighborhoods has, in the last couple of decades, made it a haunt of car thieves and even the odd mugger or two. That's kept the housing prices lower than in some tonier areas. It's also kept out the movie-industry riffraff for the most part. We lived in one of the many duplexes sprinkled throughout the neighborhood.

On our walk to the park, I was taking up quite a bit of sidewalk space—all of it to be exact. Without realizing it, I'd caused something of a traffic jam behind me, which I noticed only when a polite little voice said, "Excuse me, may we pass?"

I turned around to see a gaggle of boys, ranging in age from about six to ten, gliding on Rollerblades behind me. They looked like your basic boys, kneepads covered in mud, shirttails flying, except that their shirts were white button-downs and they wore black trousers. They also wore yarmulkes and sported long, curling sidelocks. Hasidic Jewish Rollerbladers.

Los Angeles, like New York, has a large and vibrant Hasidic community. These are the most observant Jews; they

follow the rules of Judaism to the absolute letter. They
wear traditional clothing, the men in dark suits with their
heads covered at all times. The women dress modestly, in
long dresses with sleeves past their elbows, and their hair
concealed by wigs and hats. The Hasidim follow a *rebbe*, a
spiritual leader. There are different sects that, if you are
more familiar with them than I, can sometimes be told
apart by their distinctiveness of dress; some groups of men
wear knickers or fur hats, some women wear only dark
tights and eschew light-colored stockings of any kind.

The Hasidic community is about as different from your
basic, garden-variety assimilated Jew as the Amish are
from the members of your local Episcopalian church.

Because my neighborhood is relatively inexpensive, and
because the duplex apartments are large and comfortable,
it has become home to much of Los Angeles's Hasidic
community. The neighborhood boasts a number of yeshivas
and synagogues, and it's always possible to find "a piece
herring," as my grandfather would say—except on a Satur-
day. That's when the myriad little kosher grocery stores
and markets close up tight until Sunday morning. Because
this is Los Angeles, the land of weird contradictions,
there's also a huge Honeybaked Ham store right in the
middle of the Hasidic enclave. Go figure.

I didn't have a lot of contact with the Hasidim. They
keep pretty much to themselves. The mothers rarely take
their kids to the park, although the older children do seem
to have free run of the streets—unlike the other neighborhood kids, most of whom are chauffeured by their ex-
lawyer or stockbroker moms from carefully organized play
dates to music lessons to ballet to soccer practice.

"Sorry, guys," I said, and pushed the stroller up a driveway so they could whiz past.

"Why do those boys dress so funny?" Ruby asked.

"They don't dress funny, sweetie. They're just wearing yarmulkes and *tzitzit*."

"They do so dress funny. What's a yummyka and tis tis?"

"Okay, maybe it is a little funny. A yarmulke is a little hat and *tzitzit* are those long strings hanging out of their pants. Those are special things Jews wear."

"We're Jews and we don't wear those."

"True." What to say? *That's because we're bad Jews*? I settled for something that one of the teachers at Ruby's Reform Jewish preschool would have said. "Everybody celebrates religion in a different way."

"Our way has Christmas."

"Well, that's not exactly how we celebrate being Jewish. That's more like how we celebrate being Christian. Sort of. Hey, look at that doggy!" It's nice that three-year-olds can't usually sense when their mothers are desperately trying to change the subject. Ruby and Isaac's status as children of a mixed marriage, while certainly run-of-the-mill, does bring up the occasional unanswerable question. My husband, Peter, is vaguely Protestant and decidedly nonpracticing. The closest he comes to religion is Santa Claus and the Easter Bunny. My approach to Judaism is similarly low-key, expressing itself primarily in a deep-seated identification with Woody Allen and a guilt-ridden love of bacon.

Up ahead of us the boys were gathered around a frisky golden retriever puppy on a leash. Its owner, a much-pierced, artfully bored, post-adolescent of indeterminate gender, was leaning against a tree.

One of the boys reached out his fingers and said, "Nice girl" as the dog sniffed his hand.

Another immediately piped up, "What for you tink she's a goil?" Here was this eight-year-old on Rollerblades with a thick Yiddish accent that made him sound like a pint-sized version of my great-uncle Moe.

I maneuvered the stroller around the Hasidic boys and continued up the street. On the corner of La Brea we passed a little kosher market.

"Hey, Ruby, want some gelt?" Ruby and I share a soft spot for the chocolate coins in gold foil that used to be available only around Hanukkah. You can get them year round in my neighborhood.

"Yes! Mmm!"

We walked up to the entrance of the store and I leaned forward over the stroller, trying to reach the door handle. No luck. I walked around to pull it open and then had to leap for the stroller, which was starting to roll down the sidewalk. The door slammed shut. This is the twenty-first century. By now weren't all doors supposed to glide soundlessly open, activated by heat-sensing devices? For that matter, weren't we all supposed to have personal anti-gravity packs that would make awkward double-strollers a fond memory?

For some reason, and totally out of the blue, this disap-pointment of the futuristic fantasies created in my genera-tion by *The Jetsons* made me cry. I leaned against the handles of my stroller and sobbed, inelegantly and furi-ously. I just felt so overwhelmed and hopeless, and most of all, tired. Deeply and completely tired down to my very bones. I stood there weeping while my two children stared.

"Please Mama. Don't cry," Ruby whispered. Isaac whimpered. The terrified looks on their faces sent a wave of guilt washing over me and made me cry even harder. Suddenly, the door swung open, propped by a small, sneakered foot. I wiped the back of my hand across my streaming eyes and nose and quickly wheeled the stroller through the door and into the small, dimly lit market. The store was packed with shelves overflowing with merchandise unknown to my usual grocery store: kosher canned vegetables, Israeli candies, products made by companies called Feingold and Essem and Schwartz's. I turned to thank the owner of the foot, a breathtakingly lovely teenage girl in a calf-length skirt, dark tights, a man's white Oxford shirt buttoned up to the neck and a pair of decidedly spiffy Air Jordans. She had long, dark hair plaited into a single braid down her back and the loveliest eyes I'd ever seen. They were a very dark blue, almost purple, and were fringed with thick dark lashes. A Jewish Elizabeth Taylor.

"Thanks so much," I said, gulping a little.

"You're welcome," the girl answered, in a soft voice. She looked away from my blotchy tear-streaked face and knelt in front of the stroller. "Hello there. What's your name?" she asked my three-year-old.

"Ruby," my daughter answered.

"Ruby! What a coincidence! I have a ruby ring." She showed Ruby the small gold band with a tiny sliver of a ruby she wore on her right hand.

"Bootiful," Ruby said, reaching out a finger to touch it. "My mama only has a stinky old plain ring." My daughter, Paloma Picasso Wyeth.

"That's my wedding ring, Rubes. It's supposed to be plain," I said.

"Her wedding ring has sparkling gems," Ruby answered, derisively.

"Oh, that's not my wedding ring," the girl said with a

smile. "I'm not married. My daddy gave me this for my sixteenth birthday."

"It's lovely," I said.

"Is this your little brother?" she asked Ruby.

"His name is Isaac," Ruby said. "He's a very bad baby. He cries all night long."

"Oh no. How can you sleep? Do you have to cover your ears?"

"No. He sleeps in Mama's room so he doesn't wake me up."

Suddenly, we were interrupted by a loud voice.

"Darling, what's wrong?"

I turned around to see the shop owner leaning over her counter. She was a middle-aged *baleboosteh* with round cheeks, deep-set eyes that were about half an inch too close together, and a bright blond wig perched on the top of her head. She motioned me over.

"Come here, darling. Wipe your eyes." She held out a box of tissues. I walked over to the counter, took one, and blew my nose loudly.

"I'm so sorry. This is so ridiculous. Bursting into tears like this."

"Don't be silly. Why do you think I keep a box of Kleenex on the counter? What's wrong, darling? Did something happen to you?"

"No, nothing happened. I have no idea why I'm so emotional. It's just that I'm so tired. Isaac, that's the baby, he never sleeps. He's up all night and all day. I haven't slept more than an hour straight in four months."

"Exactly like my brother Baruch! My brother Baruch didn't sleep until he was three years old," she said, with a snort.

"Oh, my G—Oh no," I said. "Please tell me this won't last three years."

"Darling, it was awful, I can tell you. And my mother, *aleha ha-shalom,* wasn't like you, she didn't have just one other little one. She had four older. And then she had two more before Baruch shut his eyes."

"Did she survive?"

"I'm telling you, none of us thought she would. I remember she said to my father, *alav ha-shalom,* 'One more day of this and Baruch and I, we go over a bridge together. Over a bridge.' She wasn't kidding, I'm telling you."

I felt my voice begin to quiver again. "I don't think I can stand three years."

Things had been a lot easier at home when Ruby was a baby. There were two of us to deal with her back then. When I'd gone back to work, Peter had even been Ruby's primary caretaker. This time, it was different. When Ruby was a baby, Peter had been writing movie scripts and had at least some control over his schedule. A few weeks after Isaac was born, Peter sold an idea for a television series to one of the networks and was currently involved in shooting the pilot. As soon as that happened, it was as though he'd disappeared off the face of the earth. He showed up just in time to go to sleep and then slept like one of the corpses in his series (better, actually), until the next morning when he woke up and rushed off. I knew I should be supportive—after all, he was supporting *us*, financially at least—but it was hard not to be ticked off. I had, for all intents and purposes, become a single mother, and I resented every second of it. I'd been happier when he was working hand to mouth.

"Darling, it sounds to me like you need some help

around the house," the shopkeeper said, handing me another tissue. "Does your mother live nearby?"

"No. In New Jersey."

"Ach. So far. What about your mother-in-law?"

"Up near San Francisco."

"Sisters? Sisters-in-law?"

"No. Nobody lives here. We're all alone." That set me off again and I buried my face in the tissue.

"Okay, okay, *mamaleh*. Enough with the crying. You need to hire a babysitter."

"I can't do that. I don't work. This is all I *do* all day. I shouldn't need any help." When I'd left work to be with Ruby, I'd fired the nanny who'd been coming in the morning to watch Ruby until Peter woke up. I was determined to do it all myself. After all, the world was full of women raising their children without professional help. Why should I be any different? But that was before I gave birth to the child who never slept.

The shopkeeper rolled her eyes at me. "Look, darling, you're clearly exhausted. All you need is a nice young girl to come spend a few hours with the baby every day so you can run some errands, maybe even take a nap. When's the last time you had a nap?"

I shook my head.

"Nu?"

I couldn't pretend the idea didn't appeal to me. I imagined myself handing Isaac to a baby sitter, just for an hour or so. Just so that I could sleep. "You know, you're right. It's not like I'm hiring a nanny. I just need someone to come in for a couple of hours so I can take a nap."

"Listen, Fraydle." The shopkeeper turned to the teenager, who had, meanwhile, taken off Isaac's sock and was tickling his toes. "You help this nice lady out. It slows down here around ten in the morning. You go over to this lady's house and help her out a couple hours."

Fraydle looked up. "But Tante Nettie, my father said I could work for you here in the store. He didn't say I could baby-sit for . . . for . . ."

Tante Nettie put up a hand. "My brother won't mind if his girl helps out a neighbor." She turned to me. "You *are* Jewish?" she asked.

"Oh, yes," I said.

"You see?" she said to Fraydle. "You'll help out a nice Jewish neighbor lady and maybe you'll show her how to light the *Shabbos* candles while you're at it. Your father will love the idea. He'll *make* you do it, I'm telling you."

"And I'll pay you!" I said. "Just tell me how much."

"Of course you'll pay her," Tante Nettie said. "You'll pay her six—no, seven dollars an hour. For two hours. From ten to noon. Every day but Friday. Friday I need her here. For the *Shabbos* rush, I need her. By the way, I'm Nettie Tannenbaum, and this is my niece, Fraydle Finkelstein."

"I'm Juliet Applebaum and I am so incredibly pleased to meet you both." I turned to Fraydle. "You'll do it?" I asked.

"Yes," the girl almost whispered.

I scrawled my name and address on a piece of paper. "Tomorrow?"

"Tomorrow," she replied, looking worried.

"Okay, enough," Nettie said. "Fraydle, run to your mama's garage and get us another case of Kleenex. This nice young lady used them all up." She cackled and poked me in the side. I laughed.

"You need anything else from the storage area, Tante Nettie?" Fraydle asked.

"Yeah, maybe another case of chocolate. I have a feeling some little girl might want some."

Ruby's eyes lit up. On our way home Isaac fell asleep, and Ruby and I felt happier than either of us had in weeks. She, because she had piles of chocolate coins in her lap, and I, because I had a nap in my future.

Three

THAT night I informed Peter that I had hired a mother's helper for a couple of hours a day. He opened his mouth, probably to remind me that every time he'd suggested the same thing, I'd insisted that since I was staying at home full time we didn't need any help with child care. I shot him a look full of such murderous venom that he clamped his lips shut.

The next morning, at precisely 9:59 A.M., my doorbell rang. I'd showered and dressed early in the morning so that I wouldn't treat Fraydle to the terrifying sight of my un-washed, morning persona. On my way downstairs I checked my shirt front quickly, to avoid a repetition of the FedEx incident. I opened the door to find my baby-sitter standing awkwardly on the front step. She was wearing the same outfit as the day before. Isaac, who was perched on my hip, reached out a hand to her and cooed.

She smiled at him and held out her arms. "Come, *motek*."

"My grandmother used to call me that," I told her. "It means sweet, right?"

"Mmm." She was busy making googly eyes at the baby.

"Be careful; he can't sit up by himself yet, so you have to sort of prop him up on your hip."

"He's nice and big," she said. "I have a sister his age and she's much smaller."

"How many brothers and sisters do you have?" I asked.

"We're eight in all. Three girls and five boys. I'm the oldest."

"My God!" I exclaimed.

She looked up, shocked at the expletive.

"I mean, wow. Gosh. That's a lot of kids."

"Not so many. There are many families with more. Ten. Sometimes even twelve."

I shuddered. "I'm barely managing with two. I can't imagine dealing with eight. Your poor mother."

"She has me to help. And my younger sister, Sarah."

"But still. It must be exhausting. Do you think she's finished having children?"

"Oh no. She's only thirty-five years old. I'm sure she'll have more."

My mouth hung open. Thirty-five? The mother of eight was only two years older than I? *Oy vay.*

I ushered Fraydle into the house and showed her around Isaac's bedroom. It, like the rest of our apartment, was full of huge piles of brightly colored, molded plastic in various stages of disrepair. Our home had started to look like the "seconds" section of a toy store.

"Do you mind if I take him out in the stroller?" Fraydle asked. "That way you can maybe sleep a little."

"Oh, that would be wonderful. He loves the stroller. Usually. Did you see it parked at the bottom of the stairs?"

"I'll find it," she said.

"He shouldn't need to eat, but if he does, there's a little bottle of expressed breast milk in the fridge. You can heat that up."

Fraydle nodded.

"Don't forget to bring extra diapers."

She nodded again.

"So I guess I'll go take a nap now."

She nodded once more.

I walked slowly back to my bedroom. I perched on the edge of the bed, wondering exactly how I was ever going to fall asleep while I was so worried about my little boy off in the hands of a complete stranger. Two hours later I woke up with a start. I'd conked out, half-sitting, half-lying on the bed, and had rather elegantly drooled all over the quilt. Wiping my mouth, I got out of bed and staggered into the bathroom. I splashed some cold water in the general direction of my face and stared into the mirror. My right cheek was covered with angry red creases and my eye was puffy. My hair had flattened out on one side and was doing its best Eraserhead imitation on the other. I halfheartedly patted at it and, giving up, wandered out into the living room. It was silent. No baby. No baby-sitter. I opened the window overlooking the front of the house and leaned out. Below, I saw the stroller, carefully covered by a baby blanket. Presumably Isaac was inside. But could he really be sleeping?

I leaned out a little farther, looking for Fraydle. She wasn't on the stoop. Panicking a bit, I leaned out farther still. Suddenly, I caught a glimpse of her standing about thirty feet down the block. She was talking to a young man in a brown leather bomber jacket. Just then, she glanced back at the stroller and saw me leaning out the window. She gave a startled little jump and said something to the man, who hurried away. She ran back to the house and I started down the stairs to meet her.

I opened the door to find her blushing furiously and apologizing.

"I'm so sorry, Mrs. Applebaum. I only left Isaac for a minute. And he was sound asleep. I could hear him from where I was. I promise you I could."

"That's fine, Fraydle. I trust that you wouldn't leave him alone. You were close enough to hear him. It's really fine. You can call me Juliet, by the way."

She seemed to calm down. "I really am sorry."

"It's okay, Fraydle. I would do it, too, I'm sure. Except, I've never actually been in the position to. How the heck did you get him to go to sleep?"

"I just walked with the stroller. That's all."

"When did he go down?"

"Right after we left. As soon as we started walking."

"You mean he's been asleep for two hours?" I was utterly and completely shocked.

Fraydle looked at her watch. "A little less, maybe. I've got to go back. My aunt is expecting me."

"No problem. Just wait a sec and I'll get my purse."

"No, no. Pay me at the end of the week."

"All right, if that's really okay with you. Fraydle?"

"Yes?"

"Who's the boy?"

To her credit she didn't say "which boy" or "nobody" or anything else teenager-like and evasive. She just got very quiet.

"Please don't tell my aunt Nettie or my parents, Mrs. Applebaum."

"Juliet. Of course I won't tell your parents. Who is he?"

She paused and then breathed, "Yossi."

"He's not Hasidic."

"No."

"Why is his name Yossi? Is he Israeli?"

"Yes."

"Is he your boyfriend?"

"No!" She sounded almost terrified.

"Really?"

"We're Verbover Hasidim. Even stricter than Lubovitch. I can't have boyfriends. I'm not allowed to have boyfriends. The only thing I'm allowed to have is a husband. A husband my parents choose for me." Her voice was low, rushed, and even a little bitter.

"You're a little young to be married, aren't you?" I asked.

"My mother was seventeen when she married my father, and I'm eighteen. I've already turned down two matches. I'm going to have to accept one soon."

"Your parents have already tried to marry you off? Are you serious?"

"Twice. I said no to both, but there's only so many times a girl can do that before she starts to get a reputation as a snob. Or worse."

Eighteen years old and already being forced into marriage and a life like her mother's—baby after baby with menopause as the only end to it. I didn't know what to say.

"I'm sorry, Fraydle."

She looked up at me, paused a moment, and then seemed to close whatever window had been opened into her true feelings. She shrugged her shoulders and said, "My parents will make a good match for me."

"Okay."

"Aunt Nettie's waiting. I gotta go."

"Okay. See you tomorrow."

"Bye bye." And with that, she ran down the path and up the block. I sat down on the stoop and enjoyed the quiet for a moment. But only for a moment. Sensing, no doubt, that he was in danger of ruining his reputation as the most obnoxious baby in Los Angeles, Isaac woke himself up and let out a howl.

Four

THAT night Isaac actually slept for three hours in a row, between the hours of 2:00 and 5:00 A.M. When I woke to the early-morning grunting that generally preceded his early-morning shrieking, I positively leapt out of bed. It's remarkable how fabulous three hours of uninterrupted sleep can feel when you're used to none at all. I scooped the baby out of his bassinet and hustled out of the bedroom so that he wouldn't wake Peter. I went into the living room, snapped on the radio, and settled in for our morning feeding and session of *Morning Edition* on National Public Radio. Isaac had gotten used to nursing to the comforting voice of Bob Edwards. Since I never got the opportunity to read the paper, my half-hour or so of listening to the radio in the early morning hours was all that stood between me and complete ignorance of world affairs.

After Isaac had sated his appetite I put him into the

Johnny-Jump-Up clamped in the kitchen doorway. He began happily leaping up and down, and I, in a sudden and rather inexplicable bit of Martha Stewart–like ambition, decided to prepare a homemade breakfast. Soon I had a pile of lovely, golden, misshapen banana pancakes warming in the oven, the table was set for three with the juice poured and the syrup heated, and the coffee was hot in the French press. I went to wake up the other members of my family.

Ruby woke, groggy and grumpy, but cheered up when I told her that pancakes were in the offing. Her father needed a little more encouragement.

"Honey! Wake up!"

Grunt.

"Sweetie. Sweetie. SWEETIE." I grabbed the pillow off his head. "Wake up! I made coffee. And pancakes!"

"Five more minutes," he mumbled, burying his head under the covers.

"Oh, c'mon, Peter. The pancakes are getting soggy."

I leaned over him and started nuzzling his neck. "Please, wake up," I whispered. Then, I plunged my tongue into his ear.

"Eeew!" he screamed, leaping about six feet in the air. "For crying out loud, Juliet, what's your problem?" He sat on the edge of the bed, digging his finger into his ear. "That is just so disgusting."

I smiled sweetly. "I made breakfast."

He looked up at me, surprised. "What?"

"Pancakes. I made pancakes."

"Wow. Okay. I'm up." Peter scratched his little potbelly, pulled on a pair of pajama bottoms, and followed me into the kitchen. We stopped in the hall and watched Ruby and Isaac. They were holding hands, and Ruby was gently bouncing the baby in the Johnny-Jump-Up. Her red curls glinted in the morning sunlight that, unusually for L.A., a city where the fog and smog don't ordinarily burn off before midmorning, streamed in through the window. Isaac had a huge grin on his face. As we watched, Ruby leaned over and kissed him on the cheek.

"Jump, Izzy. Jump jump jump," she said.

"Hey, Peach," Peter called.

She ran across the floor and leapt into his arms. "Good morning, Daddy. Look at the bootiful day."

"It sure is beautiful, honey."

We had the most pleasant meal together that we'd had in months. Since Isaac's birth, Peter and I had been behaving less like lovers and more like fellow laborers in a baby factory. And he was definitely a part-time employee. We'd gone from spending virtually all day together—Peter had always worked at night while I was asleep—to seeing each other about as much as your average married, professional couple, that is, not very much. I didn't know if it was the lack of time, or my exhaustion, or just the added pressure of another baby, but something wasn't right between us. We hadn't gone out on a date or even had a good long talk in ages. And let's not even discuss our nonexistent sex life.

"Juliet," Peter said, "you seem like yourself for the first time in months."

I smiled at him. "I feel like myself for the first time in months. No wonder authoritarian regimes use sleep deprivation as a form of torture. It's amazingly effective."

He leaned over and kissed me on the cheek. "I've missed you."

I felt a twinge of irritation. It wasn't my fault I'd been out of sorts. How would he feel if he had to spend his nights comforting a fussy baby? And hey, I wasn't the one at the studio all day and half the night. However, I was determined not to let anything ruin the mood of my lovely day. I suppressed any and all negative feelings and smiled—a stiff little smile, but a smile nonetheless.

"Is your little Orthodox girl coming today?" he asked.

"Yup. At ten. I can't wait."

Peter dressed Ruby, made her lunch, and took her to school on his way to work. I waved goodbye from the front step and then took Isaac upstairs. By a quarter to ten we were both bathed, dressed, and waiting for Fraydle.

At ten we were sitting on the front step.

At a quarter past ten we were standing at the end of the walk.

At ten-thirty we were halfway down the block.

At ten forty-five, I put the baby in his stroller and stormed off to Mrs. Tannenbaum's. When I got to the market, I saw that the door was locked and the CLOSED sign was up. I peered through the glass of the door, and spotted a young girl sitting in the back on a high stool, reading a book. I rapped a few times on the glass and she looked up. She shook her head and motioned toward the CLOSED sign. I rapped again, insistently. Finally, she got down off the stool and came to the door. Opening it a crack, she said, "She's closed today."

The girl looked like a less attractive version of Fraydle. Her hair was the same dark color and was worn in the same simple braid down her back, but it was thinner and less glossy. Her eyes were dark blue but without any of Fraydle's purplish vibrancy. Her mouth and nose were both just slightly larger than Fraydle's. But still, I was confident I knew who she was.

"Sarah?" I asked.

She looked puzzled. "How do you know my name?"

"My name is Juliet Applebaum. Your sister Fraydle

works for me. She didn't show up this morning and I came to look for her." Sarah fidgeted uncomfortably with the button on her shirt. "Do you know where she is? Can you call her for me?" She didn't answer. "I'm not mad, or anything. I just want to know if she's okay, and if she plans on coming to work today. Or ever, I guess."

Still nothing.

"Sarah," I said, sharply.

She looked up, startled. "You should talk to my father," she said.

"What? Did your father decide she couldn't work for me? Is that what happened?"

"Please, just talk to my father."

"Sarah, what's going on here?"

"Fraydle's gone."

Now it was my turn to be startled. "Gone? What do you mean, gone? Where is she?"

"She didn't come home yesterday. Everybody is looking for her right now. I'm supposed to stay in the store in case she calls or comes here."

I didn't know what to say. Suddenly, I remembered the young man in the bomber jacket. Could she have gone off with him? Could she have run away with Yossi? Should I tell her parents about seeing them together?

The shrill ring of the telephone interrupted my thoughts. Sarah snatched it up.

"Hello? No, *Abba*. She hasn't called. Okay, *Abba*. *Abba*, wait. That lady is here. The one that Fraydle baby-sat for yesterday. She came looking for her."

There was a pause.

"Yes, right now, *Abba*." She hung up the phone. "My father says come to our house right now."

I thought about it for a minute. Did I really want to get in the middle of this? What was I going to tell Fraydle's father? Fraydle had told me that her parents were planning an arranged marriage for her, a practice I thought had gone out with corsets and horse-drawn carriages. Maybe Fraydle had decided to run away rather than be forced into a marriage she hadn't chosen for herself. If that was the case, I certainly wasn't going to help her parents track her down.

Sarah had started out the back of the shop. Realizing that I wasn't following, she turned around and said, "You must come. Now. *Abba* is waiting."

"Sarah, give me your telephone number. I can't go to your house because . . . because I need to get the baby home. I'll call your father within half an hour or so." I wanted to talk to Peter before I did anything.

Sarah ran back to me and grabbed my hand. "No!" she said, almost yelling. "*Abba* said you have to come now!"

I extricated my hand from hers. "I'll call him as soon as I get home, Sarah. I've got to go now."

She shook her head frantically. "No! *Abba* said I had to bring you now. You have to come. Please. Please." She began to cry.

"Okay. Okay. I'm coming. I'm coming. Stop crying, for goodness' sake." It was clearly fear of her father and not concern for her sister that was causing this hysteria. I didn't have the heart to make her any more panicky than she was. Following the girl, I humped the stroller out the back door and down the few stairs leading to an alley.

"It's just down there." She pointed to the end of the alley. We reached the corner and turned into the fenced yard of a small stucco house. There was a small lawn and a few flowerpots with red geraniums on the long flight of steps that led up to the porch. The garage took up the first floor of the house, and the front door opened into the second floor.

I picked Isaac's stroller up in my arms and followed Sarah up the steps and through the front door of the house. Once inside, I put the stroller down and looked around. The living room was packed with bearded men in black suits and broad-brimmed hats. They were standing in little clumps, whispering to one another. I knew that shorn of their facial hair and side curls and wearing jeans and T-shirts, they could easily have been some of the many cousins and uncles with whom I'd attended bar mitzvahs and weddings, but it was almost impossible to imagine these men not garbed in their traditional attire. They looked as if they'd been wearing those coats and white stockings for two or three hundred years. As we entered, all conversation ceased as they looked silently and intently at us.

"Um, I'm Juliet Applebaum?" My voice cracked a bit. The men with their piercing eyes and unsmiling mouths made me nervous.

Suddenly, Mrs. Tannenbaum bustled out of what was most likely the kitchen and rushed over to me. She had obviously been crying; her eyes were rimmed with red.

"Come. Come," she said, grasping my hands and trying to drag me into the living room. At that moment, Isaac began to cry. I disentangled myself from her grasp and lifted him out of his stroller. Resting the baby on my shoulder, I patted his back and crooned softly to him.

"Come." Mrs. Tannenbaum pushed me farther into the room. The men backed away from us, leaving a little path for me. I knew that they were forbidden to touch me, a strange woman, who might even be in the middle of the unclean part of her menstrual cycle. A large man in shirtsleeves with a thick, unruly black beard sat on the couch in the middle of the room. He looked to be in his early to mid-forties. He wore no hat, but an oversized black velvet yarmulke covered the entire top of his head. He rose as I approached.

"This is my brother, Fraydle's papa, Rav Finkelstein," Mrs. Tannenbaum said. "Baruch, this is the woman I told you about. The nice Jewish lady who Fraydle was helping with her baby." She stepped back.

The rabbi looked at me silently. I felt intensely self-conscious in a pair of Peter's jeans rolled up at the cuff and cinched as tightly as possible, that is to say, not particularly tightly, at the waist. Thank heavens I had on a long-sleeve shirt. Too bad it had a large picture of Madonna wearing a black leather bustier.

"Hello, Rabbi. My name is Juliet Applebaum." I instinctively extended my hand, but quickly withdrew it, remembering that he could not shake it.

"You know my Fraydle, my daughter," he stated.

"Yes."

"She worked for you yesterday."

"Yes."

"You know this was without my permission. You know that she did this without telling me."

"No. No, I didn't know that." I turned to glare at Mrs. Tannenbaum, who backed away still farther, her eyes boring a hole into the faded green carpeting.

"I most assuredly did not know that," I said firmly.

"But you did not ask her if she had her father's permission to work for you. To work for a . . ." He left the sentence hanging in midair.

I was beginning to get angry. "To work for a mother with

a small child, Rabbi Finkelstein. A Jewish mother. With a Jewish child."

He gave my outfit an ostentatious and derisive look. "A Jewish mother," he spat.

Isaac began to cry.

"Excuse me," I said. "My baby is hungry. I need to go home and nurse him." I spun on my heel and walked toward the front door. Just then, a woman rushed out of the kitchen.

"No. No, please don't go." She took my arm. "Come, feed the baby in the kitchen. Come." Ignoring the men in the front room, she began dragging me into the kitchen. I couldn't shake her off without being violent, so I followed.

The kitchen was small, plain, and practical. The walls and cabinets were painted white and the only decoration consisted of dozens of children's paintings and drawings that covered every wall, every cabinet door, and the fridge. A large round table scarred by years of use was shoved into a corner. Sitting around the table and leaning against every counter were women. There were old women in stiff, discolored wigs, younger women wearing fashionable well-coiffed wigs or headscarves, and girls with long braids or hair cropped to chin-length. The room smelled warm and yeasty, like baking bread. The woman who had taken my arm was wearing a loose-fitting gray woolen dress. Her brown wig was slightly askew and her face was red and blotchy. Her large, violet, lavishly lashed eyes were bloodshot. Clearly she, too, had been crying.

"Please excuse my husband, Mrs. Applebaum. He is not used to dealing with . . . with other people. Not from our community, I mean. He is upset. We are all upset. Come through here to the back bedroom. Nurse your baby there.

We'll talk in a minute, okay? Nurse your baby and then maybe you'll tell us what Fraydle did yesterday. Maybe you'll be able to help us figure out where she is, okay?" She led me into a back room and shouted over her shoulder, "Nettie! You come sit with Mrs. Applebaum." Mrs. Tannenbaum, who had followed us into the kitchen, quickly walked into the room. Fraydle's mother backed out the door and shut it quietly behind her.

I looked around me. Mrs. Tannenbaum and I were standing in a small bedroom with a twin bed tucked into a corner. There was a desk chair against one wall. The room was dim; the only window was covered by a dark shade pulled tightly closed.

Isaac was still crying, and I sat down on the bed and quickly undid my shirt. His tears had started my milk flowing and I had soaked right through the nursing pad and my bra. My shirt had a large wet spot right around Madonna's grimacing profile. I pulled out a breast and drew Isaac close to me. He began sucking desperately. I sighed and looked up at Mrs. Tannenbaum, the woman who'd gotten me into this mess in the first place.

"You told me that Fraydle's father wouldn't mind if she worked for me. That he'd *love* for her to work for me."

She didn't answer.

"But you didn't even ask him," I continued.

"I was going to tell him, I'm telling you." She sounded defensive. "I was going to talk to him today. I came over this morning to tell him. But by the time I got here, it was already a huge *balagan*. A mess. The girl was gone. My sister-in-law was hysterical. The men were here. My brother, he's out of his mind with worry. I told him right away about Fraydle's job." She sat down next to me and gently stroked Isaac's head. "*Oy vay*, what a catastrophe this is. A complete *imglik*."

"I'm sure she'll be back," I said. "Teenage girls run away all the time. Mostly they come home right away." I couldn't help thinking of all the girls I'd seen during the years I'd practiced as a public defender. Young girls who ran away from home and ended up on the street dealing drugs, turning tricks, doing robberies with their no-good boyfriends. I didn't mention them.

"Our girls don't run away, Mrs. Applebaum. They never run away, and certainly not when they are about to be married."

"Fraydle was getting married?"

"Of course, didn't she tell you? A wonderful *shiddach*, a match. A very important New York family, I'm telling you. The boy's father leads the biggest yeshiva in Borough Park. A wonderful family. Very important."

"Fraydle didn't tell me that."

"She's a shy girl. Quiet. Maybe she didn't feel like she knew you well enough. This is a very lucky match for our Fraydle. The boy is smart, destined to follow in his father's footsteps. And not bad-looking, either. *Oy*, Fraydle. If Rav Hirsch hears of this, he'll call off the wedding, for sure. He'll never let his son marry an uncontrollable girl. *Chas 'shalom* he should hear about this. I'm telling you, it'll kill my brother if Hirsch ends the match. Kill him."

I switched Isaac to the other breast. Mrs. Tannenbaum heaved a sigh and leaned back on her elbow. "*Gevalt*. Where is that girl?"

"Did Fraydle want to get married?" I asked.

"Of course she wanted to get married. What girl would turn down a match like that? A family like that? And the boy was even good-looking. Maybe a little skinny. Maybe a few pimples. They outgrow that. What twenty-four-year-old doesn't have pimples?"

"Had she spent much time with him?"

"Rav Hirsch brought his son here a little while ago. They met, the son said yes to the match. They met again, maybe twice more. They had some time alone. I'm telling you, when I was a girl, we didn't have such luxuries. We were lucky to see the boy's face once before the wedding. Now, these children, they meet again and again. *Oy*, Fraydle. Hirsch hears about this, it will be the end."

"Has it occurred to you, Mrs. Tannenbaum, that maybe that's exactly what Fraydle might want? Maybe she took off because she doesn't want to get married."

"Don't be ridiculous. This boy is special. This family is one of the Borough Park *machers*, the elite. The father, like I said, is an important rabbi. The mother is from money. Her brothers own half of Brooklyn. This match gives my brother ties to a powerful and important yeshiva and makes Fraydle a comfortable girl. We're not so rich that she can turn her nose up at such an arrangement." The woman once again patted Isaac on the head.

He rolled off my breast with a contented belch. She reached out her arms and took him. I waited for his shriek of protest, but he seemed perfectly content to lie against her shoulder. She burped him gently.

"Do you have children?" I asked.

"No. Mr. Tannenbaum and I were not so blessed. My brother's children are like my own." She sounded a little wistful as she rubbed my baby's back with the palm of her hand. He giggled with delight as she kissed him softly on the cheek.

"You're good with him. He's not usually so affectionate with strangers."

"What strangers? He knows me. He's been in my store. We're friends. Right, Izzaleh? We're old friends."

"Mrs. Tannenbaum, I don't really know how I can help you here. I just met Fraydle. I really have no idea where she is."

"I know. Just talk to my sister-in-law. Let her ask you a few questions. Let her reassure herself that she's followed every path."

"Okay. But I'm warning you, if your brother starts yelling at me again, I'm out that door like a bat out of hell."

She looked up and gave a snort. "I like that. Bat out of hell. I'm going to use that one. You, go talk to Sima. I'll stay here with the baby."

I left them sitting on the bed, cooing at each other, and walked back into the kitchen. Once again, all conversation stopped when the women saw me. A young woman in a brown fake-Gucci headscarf patterned with backward logos hurriedly rose from her chair at the table and motioned for me to sit down. I did. A cup of tea and a plate of cookies materialized in front of me and Fraydle's mother, Sima, sat down at my side.

"The baby's okay?" she asked.

"He's fine. He's in love with Mrs. Tannenbaum."

She smiled thinly. "Nettie is good with the babies."

"Mrs. Finkelstein, I can't give you much help. I don't know your daughter very well. I met her only once before she came to work for me, and she only came to work once. I slept the whole time she was there. I didn't really get a chance to talk to her."

"Did she tell you she had plans to go somewhere?

Maybe ask your advice about where to go?" She seemed embarrassed to be asking these kinds of questions of a total stranger, but persisted. "Did you give her any money?"

"No. She didn't ask for my advice or tell me anything. She didn't even let me pay her. I was expecting to pay her today."

I felt guilty for keeping Yossi's existence a secret, as though I were lying. Before I had kids, when I'd only had the experience of being a daughter. I would naturally identify with the children in any given situation. I'd only had the experience of being a daughter. As soon as Ruby made her appearance in the world, I switched camps: Parents are always right, and even if they're not, you should listen to them anyway. But these particular circumstances were something altogether beyond the realm of normal child-parent conflict. An arranged marriage seemed, to me at least, to be almost barbaric. It was as though Fraydle's parents were offering her to the highest bidder. Her theoretical right to turn down the match certainly didn't seem to have much real effect. I could absolutely understand it if she had sought refuge in the arms of Yossi, the mysterious Israeli. I would have done the same. I wasn't going to turn her over to the parents she had run from.

"Did she maybe use the phone from your house? Did she call someone? Or meet someone?" her mother asked.

"I'm sorry I can't help you," I said firmly. I couldn't bring myself to tell an outright lie, but I felt fine about evading the question. Then I felt a stab of guilt. The poor woman was obviously distraught, just as I would be if Ruby had run off.

It occurred to me that if I could find Yossi, he might be able to either lead me to Fraydle or pass her a message. I could tell her to call her parents, to let them know that she was okay. "I'll tell you what," I said, "why don't you let me ask around the neighborhood, and if anyone has seen her, or has heard anything, I'll let you know."

She looked at me for a moment, perhaps sensing that there was something I wasn't telling her. Finally, she spoke. "Okay. You ask around." She took a piece of paper from a pad on the table and wrote down her number.

"Mrs. Finkelstein?"

She glanced up quickly. "Yes? You thought of something?"

"No, it's not that. But have you called the police? Do they know she's missing? You should file a missing persons report. They'll start looking for her."

"No! No police!" someone shouted. I jumped, startled, as did Fraydle's mother and all the other women in the room. I turned in the direction of the booming voice and saw Fraydle's father standing in the doorway.

"This is a family matter," he said, shaking a finger in my direction. "We don't need any help from your police."

"Fine. This is your business. But if you really want to find your daughter—"

"Our daughter is no longer any concern of yours. Thank you for your help. You may go now."

I looked at him, astonished by his rudeness. "I wasn't particularly eager to come here in the first place," I reminded him. "You ordered Sarah to bring me here." The women looked nervously at one another. They'd probably never heard a woman speak that way to their formidable rabbi. I rose from my chair and swept across the kitchen to the adjacent room. I held out my arms to Mrs. Tannenbaum, who gently handed a sleeping Isaac to me. I walked back across the kitchen to the doorway, where Rabbi Finkelstein stood, blocking my way out. "Excuse me please," I said.

He moved out of the way and I walked quickly to the front door and strapped Isaac into his stroller. One of the congregation who'd been silently watching my exit, a tall, broad-shouldered boy of no more than eighteen, with smooth cheeks that had obviously never needed the ministrations of a razor, held the door open for me.

"Thank you," I said. He blushed a deep red in reply.

Five

My temper cooled as I walked home, and by the time I'd dragged the stroller up the stairs to my front door I no longer wanted to knock the rabbi upside the head with a Honey Baked Ham. I did my best to put myself in his shoes. What if Ruby had run off? Wouldn't I be crazed with worry? Wouldn't I be ready to tear apart anyone who might have helped her? In my jeans and Madonna T-shirt I probably looked to Rabbi Finklestein like the personification of the evils of contemporary Los Angeles culture. If he only knew how unattractive my life must have seemed to Fraydle. Sure, I get to wear what I want and marry whomever I want, but when push comes to shove, I'm still an exhausted mother in unbecoming old clothes married to an invisible husband. Not entirely unlike her own mother. What was the difference, really? It occurred to me that one major difference between Fraydle's mother's life and my own was that she raised her kids with the help of scores of friends and relatives, all of whom piled into her kitchen to provide support in times of trouble. I was pretty much on my own.

I plopped Isaac into his Exersaucer and piled a bunch of teething rings and toys on the tray.

"Keep yourself amused for a minute, will you, kid? Mama's got to do a little detective work."

Just how was I going to go about finding an Israeli named Yossi? The only Israeli I knew was my father's cousin's son Amos, and he lived in Houston and drove an ice cream truck. I was actually contemplating calling him, when it occurred to me that my best friend, Stacy, styles herself as Los Angeles's expert on everything. It couldn't hurt to try her.

Stacy is one of those fabulous working mothers who manage to bring home the bacon and fry it up in a pan, all the while wearing a pair of Manolo Blahniks. She's a high-powered agent at International Creative Artists, the most prestigious talent agency in Hollywood. She has a kid in elementary school who not only plays soccer like every other kid in the United States but is also a math whiz and creates elaborate trigonometry programs on his home computer, just for the fun of it. And Stacy is gorgeous. Her blond hair is always perfectly done in whatever is the style of the moment, and her nails are polished with what I swear is the same nonchip substance they use to paint the space shuttle. Sometimes it's hard to remember why she's my best friend. She's so put together that she makes me feel as though I just waddled in, unwashed and clad only in a black plastic garbage bag, after a year of living in the basement of a doughnut factory. But I love her.

"Stacy Holland's office." There was a new, chirpy little

voice answering her phone.

"Hi. What happened to David?" Stacy went through assistants like pantyhose.

"Um, he moved on. Can I help you?"

"This is Juliet Applebaum. Is Her Highness around?"

"One moment please." I heard a rustling sound. "Oh, yes, Mrs. Applebaum. I'll put you through."

The phone went silent for a minute.

"Juliet! How are you?" Stacy shouted.

"New assistant?"

"Excuse me?"

"You have another new assistant."

"Why? Was she rude? Hannah, get in here!" Stacy bellowed.

"No! She wasn't rude. God, Stacy. The poor kid. I just didn't recognize her voice, that's all. You're a goddamn tyrant!"

"Never mind, Hannah. Go back to your desk. So, darling, is there a reason for this call or are you just experiencing some free-floating hostility?"

I laughed. "No, there's no reason, really. I just was wondering if you have any bright ideas on how I might track down an Israeli named Yossi."

"Yossi who?"

"I dunno. I only have his first name."

"Juliet, that's like asking me if I know a guy named Juan from Mexico. Every other Israeli is named Yossi."

"Well, how many of them can there possibly be in Los Angeles?"

"I read somewhere that the INS estimates that there are three hundred thousand Israelis living in the Los Angeles basin alone."

"Jesus Christ! Who's back home fighting the Arabs?"

"I haven't any idea. Why are you looking for this guy? Did he sell you a bum stereo?"

"No, nothing like that. I think he's my baby-sitter's boyfriend and she's kind of disappeared. I'm trying to track her down."

"Oh, no. Oh, God no," Stacy moaned.

"What?"

"Need I remind you that last time you did something like this you ended up riddled with bullet holes?"

"Don't exaggerate. Anyway, I'm not investigating a murder. I'm just trying to track down a runaway girl."

"Whatever. I refuse to be a party to this masochistic nonsense. Find your Israeli yourself."

I blew a raspberry into the phone.

"Nice, Juliet. Pick that up from Isaac, did you? Try the air-conditioning companies."

"Excuse me?"

"For your Israeli. Try calling air-conditioning companies. Andy and I just had a new air-conditioning system installed. We had four companies come out to give estimates and Israelis ran all but one. Apparently they have a lock on the industry."

"Why does that happen?" I asked.

"Why does what happen? Israeli air-conditioning installers?"

"And Indian motel-owners, and Ethiopian parking lot attendants. Does one person go home and say, 'Ibrahim! Ganesh! Come quick to America, they have a Motel 6 shortage!' "

"Juliet, I'm going back to work. You might be able to while away the hours pondering that and other metaphysical questions, but I have to put my nose to the grindstone."

"Okay. Grind away. Thanks for the help. I knew you'd know where to start looking," I said.

"*Ciao*, kiss kiss," she said, and hung up the phone.

There were five pages of air-conditioning contractors. At least a third of them had names like Uzi's, Jerusalem Air, and Givati. Did it really make sense to call one hundred air-conditioning companies on the off chance that they might have someone named Yossi working for them, who might then turn out to be the same Yossi that knew Fraydle? I decided to try the first ten names and see what happened.

Just as I began to punch in the first number, Isaac started to fuss. Almost relieved at the interruption of what would surely prove to be a futile exercise, I scooped him up and settled down in the rocker. He nursed, voraciously as usual, and I pondered my dilemma. My search for this Yossi was beginning to feel like looking for a needle in a haystack— or, rather, a sesame seed in a bagel factory. I was contemplating my next move when I heard an explosion coming from the nether regions of my little baby boy. At almost the same moment I felt something wet spreading across my lap. I leapt out of the chair and, ignoring Isaac's angry shrieks, rushed into his bedroom. Laying him on the changing table, I looked down at myself. My jeans were soaked through across the thighs. And they didn't smell pretty.

"Oh, for God's sake, Isaac," I muttered as I peeled off his overalls. "Some leakproof lining." The child had managed to produce enough poop to drench not only his diaper, but the shirt that snapped over his bottom, his overalls, and me. Swearing under my breath, I stripped him naked and dropped the filthy clothes onto the floor. He wiggled energetically while I wiped him up. Finally, realizing that the world didn't hold enough baby wipes to clean that mess, I picked him up and marched to the bathroom. I pulled off my own disgusting clothes, turned on the shower, and stepped in, holding Isaac in my arms. He startled a bit as the water hit him, but I fixed the showerhead so that a gentle spray rained down on us. Within moments, Isaac was giggling delightedly and lifting his head to the spray, opening his mouth to catch drops of water. I grabbed the soap and scrubbed both of us down, holding his slippery body in a viselike grip.

"Hey, this is fun, isn't it?" I said.

He burped in reply and snuggled up against my chest. He suddenly seemed to notice that he was in close proximity to his favorite things in the world and he began rooting around for a nipple. I stood there for a while under the warm water, holding Isaac while he nursed. As I held his silken soft body close to mine, I felt genuinely happy. Happy to be a mother. Happy to be standing in the shower with such a delightfully sweet baby. So much of being a parent is about managing, or disciplining, or getting from point A to point B. Sometimes I wonder what the point of having children is if one spends all one's time as a parent trying to herd them in the direction you need them to go, or keep them quiet or, even better, asleep. It's even occurred to me that I'd be better off with a battery-operated infant that I could play with for an hour or so each day and then toss into the closet when I got bored with its company. And then one of those sweet but rare moments happens, and I remember why I did this in the first place.

Finally, and reluctantly, I turned the water off and bundled the two of us into warm towels. As I dressed him, I noticed that Isaac actually seemed to be nodding off. Gingerly, I picked him up and tiptoed over to his bassinet. I laid him down and backed out the door. Miraculously, he slept.

"All right!" I punched a fist into the air and cheered, soundlessly. And then I remembered Ruby. I ran into the kitchen and looked at the microwave. I was late. Five minutes late. And I hadn't even left the house yet. I rushed over to the phone and called the preschool, praying that there would be someone who would answer the phone.

"Hello, Beth El Nursery School."

"Hi. Hello. This is Juliet. Ruby's mother? I am so sorry, but I completely lost track of time. I'm still home."

"Hello, Juliet. Why don't I check if there's someone here who can drive Ruby home for you."

"Could you? That would be just wonderful. Thank you so much."

The teacher was back within a minute or two.

"Juliet, everything is fine. Jake's mommy lives over on Fairfax. She's says you're right on her way home. She'll take Ruby for you."

"Thank God. Thank *you*. Wait. Wait a minute. A car seat. Ruby needs a car seat!"

"Not to worry, dear. We have one here for just these occasions. Just make sure you return it tomorrow at drop-off."

"I am so sorry. Thanks so much."

"Not at all. Not at all. Goodbye, dear."

"Bye bye." Bye bye. I sounded like a flight attendant—a stewardess on Bad Mother Airlines.

six

I took advantage of the half-hour before Ruby got home to do the laundry and call some of the air-conditioning companies. Three of the ten I tried had guys named Yossi working for them. Only one company receptionist would give me a physical description and it didn't match Fraydle's boyfriend. I couldn't remember much about how he looked, but I was fairly certain he wasn't six foot three and blond. The other two people I spoke to who acknowledged the presence of at least one Yossi agreed to pass a message on. I didn't have high hopes that if, by some miracle, the message actually got to the right man, he would call me. After all, if it was the right Yossi, and if he did know where Fraydle was, he was presumably helping her hide out. Why would he ever help a stranger locate her?

After exploring my ten dead ends, I decided to skim through the list and give it one final shot. My eyes stopped short on the *Y*'s. There, under air-conditioning contractors, was the name "Yossi Ya'ari, Lcd. Contractor. I quickly called the number. It rang twice.

"Allo?" The line was full of static and I could hear what sounded like cars driving by. A cell phone.

"Hello, can I speak to Yossi, please?"

"This is Yossi." The man spoke with a thick Israeli accent; it sounded sort of like a cross between Brooklyn and Kuwait.

"Hello. Hi. Um, are you by any chance the Yossi who is a friend of Fraydle Finkelstein?"

"Fraydle? Who?"

"Fraydle Finkelstein?" I was barking up the wrong Yossi tree, clearly.

"No. I don't know any Fraydle."

"Okay, thanks for your time." I was about to hang up when something occurred to me. "Listen, I wonder if you can help me."

"Yes?"

"I was just wondering if you might know of some place that's popular with Israelis. You know, like a restaurant or bar?"

"Why? You want maybe to find a handsome Israeli man? You don't need a bar; you need me!"

I laughed politely. "I'm trying to track down a young Israeli man named Yossi."

"I am not so old, only sixty-two! Is that good enough for you?"

My polite laugh was getting stiff. "No, I'm looking for a specific Yossi, around twenty-one or twenty-two years old."

"Not me. So sad. Listen, where does this Israeli live?"

"I'm not sure, but maybe around Hancock Park."

"Near Melrose?" he asked.

"Possibly."

"Try Nomi's on the corner of Melrose and La Brea. It's a restaurant. Every Monday and Wednesday they have there music from Israel. Very popular with the young people. Maybe you can find him there."

"Thanks! Thanks so much, Yossi."

"I hope you find your Yossi. Wait, one minute. You are not from the INS?"

"No. No. Nothing like that."

"Good. Try Nomi's. Maybe you'll find him."

I hung up the phone just in time to hear a horn beeping in front of my house. I ran down the stairs and out the door to find Ruby being extracted from a Mercedes four-by-four. The woman who was helping her out was obviously Jake's mom, but I couldn't for the life of me remember her name. She was wearing leggings, a matching sweatshirt and a pair of cross-trainers. She'd clearly just finished a workout. I glanced down at my decidedly un-aerobicized body and sighed. Someday I would find the energy to exercise. Maybe.

"Thanks so much!" I said. "I've just had the most ridiculous morning. I can't believe I forgot to pick Ruby up!"

The woman began to speak, but I couldn't hear a word she was saying. Ruby's indignant howls drowned her out.

"You forgot me!" my daughter shrieked. "You forgot me! You are a very very bad mama!"

"I'm so sorry, honey." I picked her up and hugged her. "I'm so sorry, sweet girl."

I kissed her a few times. She glared at me, and then her lower lip began to tremble.

"Oh honey, don't cry. Mama is so sorry."

With that, the tears began.

"She wasn't crying at all on the way home," Jake's mom said. "The two of them were singing the whole way."

"I believe that," I said, over the top of Ruby's hysterical head. "Thanks again, it was really nice of you."

"No problem. I live just a little farther along towards the Beverly Center. You're right on our way home. My name is Barbara, by the way."

"Of course, Barbara. Was it that obvious? I'm terrible with names."

"Me too. Brenda told me yours, otherwise I'm sure I wouldn't have remembered it either." She was probably just being polite.

"The kids sure seem to have hit it off," she said.

"That's terrific." It was a relief to know that Ruby could make friends. I've never been the best at organizing play dates. I can't plan my *own* social engagements, let alone Ruby's.

"Juliet, I was wondering, my older son goes to Milken Community School. In a couple of weeks the seventh grade is doing a production of *The Boys From Syracuse*. Would you and Ruby like to come see it with us? I think the kids will really love it."

Yeah, right after I have my fingernails pulled out, one by one. "Sure, that sounds great. Just let me know the details."

Ruby and I waved goodbye and headed up the stairs. I set her up with some markers and paper and we spent the next hour or so drawing portraits of our family. In mine, Daddy was far off in the distance, in a land called Work. In Ruby's, he was the largest figure on the page. I think we were expressing the same emotion, each in our own particular way.

That evening, long after I'd started listening for his car

in the driveway, Peter called to let me know he was going to be late. Again.

"I was really hoping to go out tonight," I said, not a little irritated.

"I'm sorry, doll. Did you have plans with Stacy? I didn't realize. Do you want me to see if I can juggle things around here?" Now that was as insincere an offer as I'd ever heard.

"No. No, it's okay," I said. "I have to go check out this Israeli restaurant. Today's Wednesday and if I don't go today, I'll have to wait until Monday."

"Come again?"

"It's a long story. I'll tell you all the details when you get home, but in a nutshell, Fraydle has disappeared and I'm hoping to bump into her boyfriend at this restaurant on Melrose. It's supposedly a big Israeli hangout on Wednesdays and Mondays."

"Disappeared? How disappeared?"

"I think she's probably run away with this guy. I'll tell you all about it when you get home. Maybe I'll just take the kids to the restaurant for dinner."

There was a moment of silence on the line. Then he said, "Juliet, you're not getting *involved* in anything are you?"

"Don't be ridiculous, Peter. I'm just trying to find my goddamn babysitter. The poor kid is probably on the run from a horrible arranged marriage. Like I said, I'll tell you all about it when you get home."

"You wouldn't take the kids any place dangerous, would you?"

"Of course not. But hey, if you're really worried, why don't you come watch them while I go out?" I knew that was a nasty thing to say as soon as I said it, but I was pretty fed up with playing the part of the brave little television widow.

"I'm not worried. And I can't leave. Things are insane right now, but you know it will mellow out as soon as the pilot is in the can."

"Yeah, maybe. Or maybe they'll buy twenty-two episodes and we'll never see you again."

There was more silence on the other end of the line. Suddenly, I regretted my snappishness. Here the guy was, trying to support us, with no help from me, and I was giving him grief.

"I'm sorry, Peter. I know you can't help it. I'm just tired. I'm always tired. Go back to work, honey. We're fine. I love you."

"You do? Because, lately, it doesn't really seem like it."

Did he really feel that way, or was he just trying to make me feel guilty?

"Oh, give me a break, Peter. I told you, I'm just tired. Of course I love you. You try waking up every fifteen minutes for four months and see how pleasant you sound."

Two could play at the guilt game.

"I know. I know," he said. "I'm sorry, too. This is just a really lousy time for both of us."

"No kidding."

"Listen, I've got to run. They're calling me. I love you."

"Me too."

"Me too, too."

Trying not to feel too miserable about the conversation, I went into the bedroom to change my clothes for dinner. My Madonna T-shirt hadn't served me very well with Fraydle's father and I needed a change of luck. I grabbed a long black skirt with an elastic waist and pulled that on over a pair of black leggings. I topped that with a freshly

laundered, white button-down shirt of Peter's. I picked up
the baby and was on my way out to the living room to get
his sister when I glanced in the mirror above my dresser.
Ugh. My hair. Somehow, during the course of the day, I'd
managed to mash down the front while, at the same time,
doing something to the back that made it look decidedly
like a third-grader's diorama of the Rocky Mountains.
Peaks and valleys. I grabbed an old black beret out of my
closet and put that on my head in what I hoped approxi-
mated a jaunty angle.

Nomi's was unprepossessing, to put it generously. The
sole decorations were a number of ancient posters of Israel
taped crookedly to the walls. There was one of Jerusalem
from the air, with the Dome of the Rock prominently fea-
tured. Another showed a laughing female soldier, securely
buckled into what looked like a parachute. The third appeared to be a view of a nondescript Los Angeles neighborhood, but the caption informed me, in bold neon, that it
was "Cosmopolitan Tel Aviv." There were about twenty
scruffy-looking Formica tables crammed closely together
facing the far right corner, where a small stage was set up
with music stands and an amplifier.

I stood hesitantly in the doorway, wondering if I should
seat myself at one of the few remaining empty tables. I
looked toward the back, where a waitress was bustling out
of the kitchen with a tray of food. She smiled and called
out something incomprehensible, pointing in the direction
of one of the tables. Within seconds a handsome young
busboy showed up holding a booster seat and a wooden
high chair. He set the booster on one of the chairs and
lifted a charmed Ruby into the seat. He then flipped the
high chair over, took Isaac's car seat from me, and settled it
snugly between the bars of the overturned high chair.

"Cool!" I said. "Where'd you learn that?"

"Babies babies, everywhere babies!" he said with an accent, pointing around the room. There were, indeed, quite a number of infants and small children in the place.

"You need menu?" he asked.

"Sure, that would be great."

He hustled off, returning after a moment with a menu and a glass of water for me, and some crayons for Ruby.

"Mama?" Ruby piped up.

"Yeah, honey?"

"I love this restaurant. This is the goodest restaurant I've ever seen."

"Even better than Giovanni's?" Peter and I have been regulars at our neighborhood Italian restaurant since before Ruby was born. Giovanni and his brother Frederico taught Ruby to say *ciao* before she even learned how to say "hello."

She paused for a moment. "No. Giovanni's is the goodest. This is the gooder."

"I'm glad you like it. Let's see what you think of the food. How about I order you a felafel sandwich and some french fries?"

"Fel fel like Daddy gets me at Eata-Pita?"

"The very same."

"Yummy."

The waitress, a petite brunette with a nice smile and two of the deepest dimples I'd ever seen, bustled over to our table. Quickly realizing that Hebrew wasn't going to go very far with us, she asked for our order in almost unaccented English. I ordered Ruby's felafel and a platter of various Middle Eastern salads for myself.

"Excuse me, miss," I said to the waitress as she finished writing down our order. "I'm looking for a guy named Yossi, darkish hair, about twenty or twenty-two years old?"

She looked at me curiously. "What do you need him for?"

"I'm actually trying to track down a friend of his, a young Hasidic girl named Fraydle. She works for me."

The waitress paused for a moment, as if she were about to tell me something. Then she said, "There aren't many Hasidim who come here. Nomi's is kosher, but not kosher enough, if you know what I mean."

I didn't, but I decided it wasn't important.

"There's music tonight, isn't there?" I asked.

"Every Wednesday and Monday. Look for your friend tonight. They all come in to hear the music."

I thanked her and scanned the room. There were lots of young men with Yossi's short haircut. There were even a few wearing similar brown leather jackets. None of them looked familiar, though.

The truth was, I didn't have a lot of faith in my ability to recognize Fraydle's Israeli, even if he should walk into the room. Eyewitness identification is notoriously unreliable. When I'd been a federal public defender I'd represented people in cases where every single eyewitness had provided a detailed description of the perpetrator—each one completely different from the others. One person would insist that the bank robber had blond hair and was six foot two. Another would swear that a Filipino dwarf had committed the crime. More than one witness usually meant that my client had a fighting chance. The real problem was when there was only one. It was virtually impossible to convince a judge to let me present expert testimony on the problems with eyewitness identification. Even if the judge did let me put a couple of scientists on the stand, juries never could get beyond their reaction to the bank teller who'd pointed a trembling finger at my client, whispering, "His face is burned into my mind."

I knew firsthand just how often eyewitnesses made mistakes. In law school my evidence professor had started class one day with a whispered discussion with a strange man who then left the room. An hour later she stopped, mid-lecture, and asked us to provide a physical description of the man. I thought he was about six feet tall or so, and I was absolutely positive that he was a young Latino man in his early twenties. I knew that he was wearing a blue windbreaker and khaki pants. I raised my hand and described the individual, absolutely certain that I was correct. A good half of the class agreed with me. My professor then walked to the door and opened it. In walked the man. He was a light-skinned black man who looked about thirty years old. He was a good deal shorter than six feet, but looked taller standing next to my petite professor. He was wearing a denim jacket and a pair of stonewashed jeans. I'd been absolutely wrong. And worse, the sheer force of my conviction had swept many of the other eyewitnesses along with me.

For all I knew, Yossi would turn out not to be the medium-height, brown-haired Israeli I remembered, but rather an eighty-year-old Inuit in a wheelchair.

While I pondered this and other challenges of detection, Ruby grew bored with her crayons and Isaac lost patience with his car seat. The next few minutes were taken up with bouncing him on my lap and trying to entertain her with a story. Finally, the food arrived. Ruby tucked into her felafel with vigor and I popped Isaac on my breast, covered his back with a napkin, and stared at the vast plate covered with multicolored salads that the waitress set before me. There was easily enough food for three hungry men or one nursing woman. I almost groaned with delight as I scooped up garlicky hummus with warm pita.

I was so engrossed in cramming as much food into my mouth as I could before Isaac finished nursing that I almost forgot the object of my search. Luckily, I had stopped for a breather when a group of young men walked into the restaurant. From across the room I heard a voice call out, *"Shalom Yossi, Yiftach! Ma ha-inyanim?* What's up?" Any one of the four or five guys could have been my particular Yossi. They were all of short to medium height with close-cropped, brown hair. Two were wearing bomber jackets. "Yossi!" I said loudly.

One of the young men turned to look at me. He pointed to his chest and frowned as if to ask, Who, me?

Of all the felafel joints in all the towns in all the world.

"Yossi?" I said again.

He walked over to me. "Do I know you?" he asked. His voice was soft with just the slightest trace of accent.

"I think you know a friend of mine, Fraydle Finkelstein?"

He stiffened for a moment and looked at me more intently. "Do I know you?" he asked again.

"My name is Juliet Applebaum. Fraydle was watching my baby the other day? On Orange Drive?"

"We did not meet."

"No. No, we didn't. But Fraydle told me all about you." He looked doubtful.

"Well, maybe not all about you. She told me that you guys are friends."

He smiled ruefully. "Friends. Yes, we are friends, I suppose."

"Yossi, would you sit down a minute so that we can talk?"

"I'm sorry. I cannot help you. I know her only a little. Just from the neighborhood." He turned his back to me and began to walk across the floor.

"Yossi!" I was almost shouting.

He turned back to me. "Please. I don't know what you want from me. I barely know this girl. We talk once, maybe twice. I did nothing wrong."

I looked at him. What made him assume that I was accusing him of anything?

"Do you know where Fraydle is?"

"What do you mean? She is where she always is. She is with her father. The rabbi." He fairly spat the words out.

"Actually, that's just where she's not. She hasn't been home since yesterday." It suddenly occurred to me that I hadn't spoken to Fraydle's family all afternoon. For all I knew, she was back home safe and sound.

"At least, she hadn't come home as of this morning," I continued.

Either Yossi was an accomplished actor or he was genuinely surprised at what I'd said. He pulled a chair over from another table and sat down between Ruby and me.

"Hey!" my daughter cried. "This is our table!"

"Ruby, this is Yossi. Mama just has to talk to him for a minute. Eat your felafel."

Ruby listened to me for once and turned back to her dinner. At that moment, Isaac gave a belch and I switched him to the other side. Yossi studiously avoided looking at my exposed breast.

"You said Fraydle is not home?" he asked.

I recounted to him how she'd failed to show up for work and my subsequent experiences with her father. "Not the most easygoing of men," I said.

"I have not met him. Your name is Juliet?"

"Yes."

"Juliet, this is not good. This is not like Fraydle to go away. She is not, how do you say, sophisticate?"

"Sophisticated."

"Yes, sophisticated. She is not. She has not spent a night away from her parents in her life. She would not just go away."

"And you have no idea where she is?" I was suspicious. After all, the first thing this guy had done was proclaim his innocence. And that was before I'd told him there might be something for him to be guilty of.

"I? Is that what you think? That she is maybe with me? That is crazy. I know this girl only a little bit."

"So you said. But you do know her enough to know she isn't sophisticated. Right?" He didn't answer. "Yossi," I said, "is Fraydle your girlfriend?"

"No! No! Nothing like that. I know her from the neighborhood. I told you this!" He shook his head angrily. "None of this is important. Where is she, that is what is important. You said you did not speak to them, to her family, this evening?"

"No. I haven't."

"So maybe she is at home." With that, he got up to leave.

"Wait. Yossi. Please wait. Let me just call her mother and see if she's home. If she is, fine. I won't bother you anymore. If not, then don't you think we should try to figure out where she might be?"

He looked at me for a moment, and then, shrugging his shoulders, sat back down at the table.

Ruby mumbled something incomprehensible from around a mouthful of fries.

"Just a minute, peach. Mama's got to make a phone call," I told her.

Reaching around Isaac's head, I dug in my purse for my cell phone and the scrap of paper with the Finkelsteins' phone number. I punched in the numbers. The phone rang only once.

"Hello? Fraydle?" a voice shouted into the phone. She wasn't home yet.

"No, this is Juliet Applebaum. Is this Rabbi Finkelstein?"

"Mrs. Applebaum. Yes. You have news of my daughter?" I could tell that I was not high on the rabbi's list of desirable conversation partners. I could also tell that he was desperate for news of his child.

"No, no, I'm terribly sorry, Rabbi. I was just calling to find out if she'd come home."

"No." And he hung up.

I stared dumbly into the phone receiver. "He hung up on me!" I announced.

Yossi didn't look surprised. "She is not home," he said, rather than asked.

"No."

He shrugged his shoulders. "Well, I don't know where she is."

"Exactly what are you and Fraydle to each other?" He didn't answer. "I know that you don't think this is any of my business, but maybe we can work together to figure out where Fraydle has gone." He remained silent. "Is it that you're afraid I'll tell her parents about you two? Is that it?" Silence.

"Hey, mister! My mama asked you something!"

"Shh! Ruby!"

Yossi looked at me for a moment and then, his face pale, he stood up again. "I cannot help you. I know her only a little bit. From the neighborhood," he repeated and made as if to walk away.

"Wait, Yossi. Let me give you my phone number, in case you think of anything. He shrugged his shoulders and stuffed the card I handed him into his pocket without looking at it.

"What's your last name?" I asked.

"Zinger," he said, turning on his heel and walking across the restaurant to the table where his friends were sitting.

"I want to go home, Mama. I want to see Daddy," Ruby whined.

"Okay, honey," I said. I hustled the kids out of the restaurant and into the car and, within an hour, had them both bathed and ready for bed. Ruby was out like a light as soon as her head hit the pillow. Isaac, as usual, was ready to rock and roll until the wee hours.

I took him into my bed and faked sleep, hoping to trick him into following suit. He was unimpressed. He lay in the crook of my arm, grunting and waving his arms about, his fingers gracefully outstretched like a miniature Thai dancer. After a futile ten minutes or so of playing possum, I gave up.

"So, what do you want to do?" I asked.

"I don't know, what do you want to do?" I answered in a squeaky baby voice.

"I don't know, what do you want to do?" *Et cetera*.

This scintillating exercise was interrupted by Peter's arrival.

"Hey," he called as he thumped up the back stairs.

"Hey," I called back.

"Are you still up?"

"No. I'm asleep. Can't you tell?"

Peter walked into the bedroom, stripping off his clothes as he crossed the worn wooden floorboards. In seconds he was next to us in bed, clad only in his boxer shorts.

"Hi, Isaac," Peter said, scooping the baby up and buzzing him on his belly. Isaac giggled.

"Hi, Daddy," I said in my squeaky voice.

"Did you guys have a good day?"

"Not really."

Peter pushed a long curl out of his eye. "Me neither."

"You go first," I said, rather generously, if I do say so myself.

"Oh, you know, just the usual garbage. The studio guys are insisting that the special effects are too expensive for TV and the director is threatening to quit unless they're left in. Blah blah blah. I swear to God, if it weren't for Mindy, I'd be going out of my mind."

I felt a flash of jealousy. The producing partner Peter's agency had set him up with was a woman of about my age with the unlikely name of Mindy Maxx. She was blond and brilliant and weighed seventeen pounds.

"And what did Maximum Mindy do today?"

Peter laughed perfunctorily. "She's really adept at handling those network drones. She keeps them in check but somehow convinces them that they're in charge. She's amazing."

"So you've said before."

He was oblivious to my sarcasm. "You do remember that we're going to her house for dinner tomorrow night, don't you?" he asked.

I hadn't remembered. "Oh God, is that tomorrow? Peter, I totally forgot. I didn't set up a baby-sitter. And Fraydle, the girl who was supposed to sit today, has disappeared. I don't know where I'd begin to find someone to watch the kids."

"I figured. That's why I found someone."

"*You* found a baby-sitter? What are you talking about? How did you find a baby-sitter?"

"Well, actually, it was Mindy's idea. Her assistant, Angelika, is going to do it."

"Angel-eeeka? Who's Angelika? We can't just let some total stranger take care of the kids." What was he thinking? Did he really believe I'd leave my kids with someone I'd never met?

"She's not a total stranger. I've known her for months—since we started developing the series. She's a nice young kid, a year or two out of college. She went to Yale, like Mindy."

"Oh, well, if she went to Yale, by all means." I was being snide. I'm a Harvard girl, after all.

"Juliet, do I need to remind you that you left Isaac with some girl you met once in a grocery store?"

That shut me up, for a moment.

"It'll be fine," Peter continued. "Angelika is a sweet kid and she's very responsible. Ruby will love her; she's got a stud in her tongue."

"Oh, well, why didn't you tell me that to begin with? Sure, no problem, as long as she's heavy into self-mutilation. I mean, who would ever want a baby-sitter who couldn't set off a metal detector or two?"

Peter sat up and lifted Isaac up over his head, zooming him around like an airplane.

"She's a nice kid," he said.

I gave up. "I'm sure she is. Ruby will love her." I sighed. "Don't get the baby all revved up. I'm trying to convince him that it's bedtime."

"Okay." Peter brought Isaac in for a landing and handed him to me.

"Why was your day so bad?" he asked, finally.

I launched into the tale of Fraydle's disappearance. I had

just started telling him about my conversation with Yossi when I noticed that he'd fallen asleep.

"I love you, too," I whispered. I looked over at Isaac, who smiled at me. At least *he* cared what I had to say. "C'mon, buddy. Let's let Daddy get some rest."

Seven

PETER was gone by the time Isaac and I got home from driving Ruby to school the next morning. My darling husband had left a note on the kitchen table.

Sorry I crashed last night. I'll be home early to get dressed for Mindy's. Why don't you go buy something fabulous to wear? It'll make you feel better.

"Better? Why do I need to feel better? I feel just fine, thank you." I muttered to myself as I crumpled the note. I had already decided to go by Mrs. Tannenbaum's store. I wasn't up to facing Fraydle's father, but I wanted to find out if Fraydle had come home. Afterwards, if we had time, Isaac and I could hit the Beverly Center and try to find something to wear to Marvelous Mindy's dinner party.

I drove the block and a half to the kosher grocery and

parked in front of the store. It was open. Measuring the distance between my car and the shop at about ten feet, I decided it was safe to leave the baby in the car. I opened his window a crack, hopped out, and went to the door of the shop. Poking my head inside, I called out to Fraydle's aunt. "Nettie? It's Juliet Applebaum."

She stood behind the register, ringing up the purchases of an elderly woman wearing a wig that appeared to be made out of molded plastic.

"Hello, darling. No word yet," Nettie said, looking up at me and shaking her head.

"Nothing?" I asked.

"Nothing."

I glanced out at Isaac, who sat, undisturbed, just as I'd left him. "I can't stay," I said. "Isaac is in the car. I was just hoping . . ." I let the sentence trail off.

"We're all hoping."

The customer looked up curiously. "What hoping?" she asked, in a thick Yiddish accent.

"Nothing, dear," Nettie reassured her. She gave me a warning glance over the top of the woman's head. I nodded and waited in the doorway, where I could watch Isaac. He was busy trying to fit both fists into his mouth.

In slow motion, the old woman packed her purchases into a net bag and crammed that into an incongruous, pink suitcase on wheels emblazoned with the words "Going to Grandmas." Finally, after about twelve hours, she trundled past me and out the door. Nettie came out from behind the counter.

"Come, we'll go stand next to your baby. *Chas v'shalom* someone should steal him out of the car."

Suitably rebuked, I followed Nettie to the car. I leaned against the front passenger door, watching her as she made goo-goo eyes at Isaac. She tickled him on his belly and spoke to him in Yiddish. The woman clearly had been born to be a grandmother. It seemed a cruel twist of fate that she'd been robbed of her chance to have children, let alone grandchildren.

"Nettie, has your brother called the police yet?"

She shook her head. "No. Baruch says we'll find her ourselves."

I shook my head, frustrated at the man's obstinacy. "And Fraydle's mother agrees with this? She's willing to let days and days pass without going to the police? For crying out loud, Nettie. What if she *hasn't* run away? What if something has *happened* to her? You could be making a terrible mistake by waiting."

Nettie whirled around to face me, her eyes flashing. "You think I don't know this? You think I don't imagine that girl dead somewhere? Or kidnapped? What do you think? I don't care? Her mother doesn't care? We don't love her? Is that what you think?"

"Of course that's not what I think. I know you love her. That's why this refusal to call the police doesn't make sense to me. It's almost as if her father doesn't want her to be found."

"Pah!" She flung her hand at me in a dismissive gesture. "What do you know? The poor man does nothing but look for her. He drives all over this city looking for her. I'm telling you, he hasn't slept since she left. The only thing he wants in the world is for her to come home."

I was silent for a moment. Nettie obviously believed what she was saying. And maybe she was right. Maybe Rabbi Finkelstein was doing everything he could to get his daughter back. And maybe he wasn't.

"I have to go," I said finally. "You'll call me if you hear anything?"

"Yes. I'll call you," Nettie said. She leaned into the car and gave Isaac a wet kiss on the cheek. He grabbed her wig and tugged it askew.

"*Motek*," she said, and patted it straight again. "A lovely boy you have, Mrs. Applebaum. Take care of him."

"I will," I said softly. I reached out and hugged the sweet older woman. She held me close for a moment and then, sniffing back tears, walked back into her store. I watched her go and then walked around to the driver's side of the car, got in, and started the engine.

"Okay, buddy, let's go to the mall," I said to Isaac as I pulled onto Beverly Boulevard. "I hear Macy's has opened up a Rotund Petites department. I'm sure it's just chock full of fabulousness."

Eight

OUR shopping trip was the exercise in humiliation I had come to expect from department stores. While my body had expanded well beyond a size ten, my eyes seemed to have gotten stuck at about a six. I took dress after dress off the rack and into the dressing room, only to find that they would fit provided I had time for a spot of liposuction. I seriously considered the plastic surgery before dumping my reject pile on a salesgirl who had been condescendingly watching my pathetic attempts.

"Ma'am, why don't you check out our large size collection? It's on the third floor, next to housewares."

I glared at her and stomped away. My dramatic exit was somewhat hampered by the fact that I got Isaac's stroller stuck on the corner of a display table. As I jerked it loose, I sent a pile of miniscule cashmere sweater sets flying.

"Sorry," I muttered to the salesgirl and hustled off across the store.

I was morosely making my way toward the escalator when my eye was caught by a mannequin wearing a pair of heavy satin pants in midnight black and an almost architectural shirt made of some kind of shiny gray fabric.

"Now, that's gorgeous," I said to Isaac. I wheeled him over to the mannequin and lifted up the price tag on the shirt. "Whew!" I gasped. The tag read $450. My first car cost less than that. The pants were a bargain at a mere $250.

"It's so hard to find something that fits when you're nursing, isn't it?"

I spun around to the source of the comment. An older woman in a beautifully tailored suit smiled at me.

"Impossible," I agreed. "Absolutely impossible."

"What's terrific about these pants is that they have an elastic waist. Very forgiving. The cut is slimming, too." She lifted up the shirt to show me the waistband of the slacks. "And the top is cut very full across the chest. Would you like to try it on?"

"You work here?" How could the same store that employed the snotty little twig who'd "helped" me earlier also have hired this lovely woman?

"Indeed, I do. In *couture*."

"Ah, *couture*," I said. That explained the price tag.

"Would you like to try it? If you decide you like it, we can shorten the slacks for you while you shop."

I paused for a moment. I had never in my life spent that much money on a single outfit, not even my wedding dress. I'd bought that at a sample sale for ninety-seven dollars. Ninety-seven dollars and the black eye I'd gotten when I yanked it out from under the sweaty fingers of another bargain-hunting bride.

"It *is* expensive," she said, reading my mind. "But it's beautifully made. It's a fabulous outfit."

She said the magic word. I was under strict orders to find fabulousness at all costs. "Okay, I'll try it."

Ninety minutes later, Isaac and I were on our way home, our trunk loaded down with the satin pants, gray shirt, and the astronomically expensive black sandals with silver buckles that I simply had to have to go with the outfit.

"I *am* fabulous, aren't I?" I asked my baby as we zipped through the streets of Los Angeles on our way to pick Ruby up at preschool.

That afternoon, I popped an Elmo video into the VCR for Ruby, mentally apologizing to the American Academy of Pediatrics, who had just informed me, via NPR, that I was doing incalculable damage to my child by allowing her to watch TV. I strapped Isaac into his Baby Bjorn and began to pace back and forth. As long as I was moving, the baby was quiet. I'd spent the day worrying more about my appearance than about Fraydle and I was feeling guilty. I was also certain that Fraydle's father was never going to find her, no matter how hard he was looking for her. I debated calling the police, but realized that without the Finkelsteins' cooperation, I wouldn't get very far. Chances were that she had just taken off, probably to avoid a marriage to someone she didn't love.

I needed to find her myself.

Even at the time, I knew my involvement with Fraydle was a little crazy; certainly it was out of proportion to how well I'd known the girl. But for some mysterious reason I felt a sense of responsibility toward her. Maybe she re-

minded me of myself at her age. Maybe her plight activated the do-gooder complex that had lain dormant since
I'd left the federal public defender's office. Maybe I just
needed to concentrate on something other than how utterly
and completely exhausted I was.

I hadn't expected Yossi to call, and he hadn't surprised
me. His evasiveness was certainly suspicious, but short of
calling the cops and telling them that first of all I had a
missing person to report and second of all I felt a little uncomfortable about the veracity of an Israeli friend of the
disappeared, I wasn't sure what I could do.

I needed some advice and I knew just who would give it
to me. I picked up the phone and, continuing to bounce
Isaac up and down on my chest, called the federal public defender's office, my old stomping ground. The secretary to
the investigators' unit put me on hold and I waited for Al
Hockey to get off his butt and answer the phone. Al had
been working as an investigator for the federal public defender ever since he'd retired after taking a bullet to the gut
in his twenty-fifth year at the L.A. police department. Re-
tirement hadn't agreed with him, and he always said that
getting people out of jail wasn't all that different from putting them away, just a little bit harder. During my time as an
attorney in that office, we'd been an unstoppable team. I
owed every one of my "Not Guilty" verdicts to his tireless
footwork. Al possessed the miraculous ability to pluck an
alibi witness out of thin air.

"If it isn't my favorite private eye! Juliet Applebaum,
how are your bullet holes?"

"Fine, Al. And yours?"

"Just fine. What borderline illegal activities do you have
in store for me today?"

"Illegal? I'm outraged. Truly outraged. When have I ever asked you to do anything illegal? Unethical, maybe. Illegal, never."

"A rather fine distinction. What do you want now?" he asked.

"Missing person's case," I replied. I told him the story about Fraydle's disappearance.

"Sounds to me like she pulled a runner, Juliet."

"Yeah, that's what I think, too, but there's always the chance, however slight, that it may be more serious, and it makes me nervous that the cops don't know about it."

"You could always call them."

"I suppose so, but I'm worried about alienating the parents. I'm just wondering if there's a way I can unofficially find out if any girls have turned up."

"Turned up where, the morgue?"

That stopped me in my tracks. I suppose that's what I meant, but I hadn't put it so bluntly even to myself.

"Well, yeah. The morgue or a hospital or something. I suppose I could call every hospital in the city, and every morgue for that matter, but I figured you might know an easier way to do this."

He thought for a moment. "I could ask one of my buddies from the LAPD to check on any Jane Does."

"That would be wonderful. What do you need to know?"

"A general physical description, age, the neighborhood she lives in, that kind of thing."

I gave Al the information and made him promise to call me by the next day with whatever he'd found out. I'd done what I could that day. And anyway, Elmo was almost over.

Nine

I was definitely not ready to go out when Peter came home. In fact, Ruby and I were both covered in flour and Isaac was in his bouncy seat, looking like a little Abominable Snowman. We'd decided to bake cookies, but had never got past the dough stage. My mother had called in the middle of our project and I'd had to spend fifteen minutes explaining to her why it was that Peter and I couldn't put his project on hold, load up the kids, and hightail it out to Jersey for a week. Or two. Or six.

"Hey, family," Peter said when he walked in the kitchen.

"Hey, Daddy," Ruby and I answered, in unison.

"Is this fabulous enough for you?" I asked, pointing at my dirty sweatshirt.

He smiled. "No, but this is." He jumped across the room and wrestled me to the floor, pulling the sweatshirt off.

Ruby, not one to be excluded from a wrestling match, leapt on top of us.

We rolled around the floor for a minute or two, laughing and shouting. Suddenly I noticed that Isaac was squalling.

"Party pooper," I said, as I got to my feet and picked him up. "We were just having fun, little guy."

"Hey, give him here," Peter said, getting up off the floor and brushing flour off his pants. "Come here, buddy. Say hi to Daddy."

Ruby began working herself into an apoplectic fit when she realized that her beloved father was actually paying attention to the usurper.

"Everybody, quiet!" I shouted. "Okay, you"—I pointed to Peter—"clean up the kitchen. You"— I looked at Ruby— "come help Mama get dressed for a party."

"I don't want to help you, I want to be with Daddy," she howled.

"Fine, whatever, Baby Electra. Help Daddy clean up. I'm going to take a nice hot bath."

AFTER my bath I slipped my new outfit out of the garment bags Macy's had so thoughtfully provided. No tacky paper shopping bags when you shop *couture*. The pants felt cool and slippery against my skin. The shirt looked, if anything, better than it had in the dressing room. I felt downright attractive for the first time in months. I carefully applied some makeup and put on my most expensive earrings, a pair of diamond studs Peter had given me when Ruby was born. I was admiring myself in the mirror when Peter and the kids walked into the bedroom.

"Wow," Peter said.

"You asked for fabulous."

"And that's what I got. You look great."

"Thanks, honey." I kissed him on the cheek and took the baby from him. He stripped off his shirt and put on a clean one. He brushed off his khakis and yanked a jacket out of his closet. I sighed. It's so much easier to be a man.

Angelika, the baby-sitter, showed up at the house with a bag full of colored paper, kid's scissors, glue, markers, and glitter. "I thought we could make our own greeting cards," she said. Ruby looked like she'd died and gone to heaven.

Peter and I left them engrossed in their project, with Isaac happily bouncing in his Johnny-Jump-Up.

"So what kind of party is this?" I asked as we drove down Beverly Boulevard toward Mysterious Mindy's Benedict Canyon house.

"What do you mean what kind of party?" Peter asked.

"You know, is this a normal people's party with, like, sour-cream-and-onion dip and a bunch of friends, or is this a Hollywood, catered kind of party with valet parking?"

"I dunno. It's dinner. It's a dinner party."

"Okay, well is it a 'come on over and I'll hand you a big bowl of chili and my grandmother's cornbread' kind of dinner party or is it a 'Suzette is serving our first course, Maryland crab cakes in a delicate saffron remoulade roux' kind of dinner party?"

"Look, Juliet." Peter turned to me. "Mindy is a friend of mine. And a colleague. My relationship with her means a lot to me. I'd really appreciate it if you'd lose the attitude."

"Professional or personal?"

"What?"

"Which means a lot to you, your professional relationship or your personal relationship?"

He looked at me for a minute and then back at the road. Neither of us said anything for a little while. Then I spoke. "Sorry."

"It's okay. I'm sorry, too." But it didn't really seem to be okay, and I didn't believe that he actually knew what he was apologizing for. Nor did I, in all honesty.

We pulled into the driveway of a 1940s bungalow that had obviously had a major face-lift sometime in the past few years. A line of young women in black vests emblazoned with the logo "Valet Girls" stood ready at the doorway. Peter handed the car keys to one and she leaped into the driver's seat and zipped off. So, it was that kind of a party.

The house was larger than it looked from the outside and decorated within an inch of its life. The style was a sort of eclectic Arts & Crafts with a few gorgeous old pieces that probably had the name Gustav Stickley carefully stamped under a drawer or behind a back panel. Each brightly colored kilim pillow and artful knickknack was in just the right spot. On the walls were a number of large black-and-white photographs in beautiful wooden frames. One, a photo of a pair of lovely young girls bathing in the ocean, looked to my untrained eye like a Sally Mann.

"This place is amazing!" I whispered to Peter.

"I know," he whispered back. "You should see the kitchen. It's gorgeous."

What the heck? How did he know what the kitchen looked like? I was getting ready to ask him, or punch him in the stomach, when the impeccably decorated owner of the impeccably decorated house glided up.

Magical Mindy was wearing a sleek black pantsuit and a white blouse with French cuffs that protruded from her coat sleeves and dangled over her fingers. She had on black stiletto heels that, in case we missed it, had the name Prada embroidered on the side. Her toenails were painted electric blue and her carefully tousled and highlighted hair fell in luxurious curls down her back. I hated her.

"Hello! Juliet! It's so wonderful to see you again. You look fabulous!"

I smiled, perhaps a bit grimly. "So do you, Mindy. Absolutely."

We stood there awkwardly for a moment, trying to think of something to say, and then Mindy turned to Peter. "Pete, listen, there's a kid here that I want you to meet. He's a hot new actor and I think we should consider him for one of the mid-season roles. He's hip-pocketed at CAA and I think he's about to shoot through the stratosphere."

"Terrific," Peter said. He turned to me. "I'll be right back, okay?"

"Sure, no problem." I answered, inwardly seething. Who, exactly, was "Pete" and who did he think I was going to talk to at this event?

I grabbed a glass off the tray of a passing waiter, plopped myself down on an overstuffed sofa, and sipped at my wine, feeling sorry for myself. Nobody talked to me, although who could blame them? I looked about as much fun as a colicky baby. After what felt like an hour but was probably no more than ten minutes, Peter came back. He sat down next to me.

"You're having a terrible time, aren't you?" he said.

"No, I'm having a great time. Really."

"Baloney."

"Okay, it's baloney. I'm sorry. It's just that I don't really know anyone. Everyone at this party is from TV or something. None of our friends are here."

"Why don't you try to meet some people? Make some new friends."

Like that was so easy.

I said, "You're right. You're totally right. Why don't you introduce me to some of the people you work with?"

Peter popped off the sofa and extended his hand to me. I took it and he hauled me to my feet. "Okay, let's go meet some folks."

"Okay," I said, not overly thrilled at the prospect.

After about twenty minutes I inwardly vowed that I would kill the next person who ardently shook my hand and said, "I am such a big fan of your husband's." Fan? Please. Those jaded Hollywood types hadn't been fans of anything since they had Shawn Cassidy's picture taped inside the doors of their lockers in sixth grade.

I was thinking up some snappy insult for the next "fan" when Peter leaned over and whispered in my ear, "Honey, you're leaking."

"I'm what?" Then I looked at my shirt. A large circle of damp was slowly spreading over the incredibly expensive fabric. I'd forgotten to put a breast pad in my bra.

"Oh, God," I said, and rushed out of the room. I couldn't find an unoccupied bathroom so I tore into the kitchen, dodging a caterer or two, and found a roll of paper towels. I tore off a handful and shoved them down my shirt.

"Are you okay?" I heard a woman's voice ask. I looked up into the dimpled face of the waitress who had served the kids and me at Nomi's, the Israeli restaurant. She was dressed in black slacks and a white caterer's jacket.

"I'm fine. Just leaking. You work at Nomi's, don't you?"

She plucked a dishtowel out of a pile of neatly folded cloths sitting on the counter and dampened it with San Pelligrino mineral water. "Try this," she said, handing it to me. "Seltzer gets out anything. Yes, I work at Nomi's. I also do catering jobs sometimes. For extra money. You came into the restaurant last night, right?"

I nodded and dabbed at the stain on my shirt. As far as I could tell I was just making a small wet spot into a larger one.

"You talked to Yossi," she continued.

"Yes."

"About his girlfriend."

My head shot up. Girlfriend? "You know her?" I asked.

The young woman shrugged her shoulders. "A little bit. One minute." She turned to the stove, a huge Viking range with an eight-burner cook-top and an oven that looked like it could roast six or seven Thanksgiving turkeys at the same time. Donning a pair of oven mitts, she reached into the oven and took out a cookie sheet of miniature *spaniko- pita* that she began to carefully arrange on a cut-glass tray.

"So, you know Fraydle?" I pressed.

"The Hasidic girl? I'm not her friend, but I have seen her sometimes."

"In the restaurant?"

"Oh, no. I don't think she would ever eat at Nomi's. No, in my building." She finished arranging the hors d'oeu- vres. "I'll be right back," she said, and headed out the kitchen door.

I busied myself with my shirt, doing my best to dry the fabric. It occurred to me that the warm oven might help in that endeavor, so I opened the door and crouched down close to it.

"What are you doing?" the waitress asked as she came back into the kitchen.

"Just trying to get my shirt dry."

"Oh, good idea," she said. She squeezed by me and busied herself at the kitchen counter, taking the plastic wrap off a tray of sushi.

"You were telling me about Fraydle," I reminded her.

"Yes. The Hasidic girl. Yossi and I live in the same building, so I see her sometimes. Just passing in the courtyard, you know?"

Well, that certainly gave the lie to Yossi's claim about just seeing Fraydle "around the neighborhood."

"Are you friendly with Yossi?" I asked.

She shrugged. "Once. Maybe. I knew him from the army. You know, in Israel?"

"You were in the army?" She didn't look like a soldier. She looked like a typical Melrose Avenue babe.

"It's not such a big deal. We all go to the army in Israel. I was a secretary in his unit. So I knew him." There was something about her tone that bothered me.

"What kind of unit?"

"Excuse me?"

"What did you guys do in the army?"

She paused, and looked up at me. "Why do you ask that question?"

"No reason. I was just curious." And I wanted to find out if Yossi had any Israeli military training that would, say, allow him to spirit an eighteen-year-old girl out of her home without a trace.

"We were in the paratroopers."

"Wow. You jumped out of planes?"

"I jumped only once. But that's what the men did, yes."

Changing the subject, I said, "You know, we haven't even introduced ourselves. I'm Juliet Applebaum."

"Anat. Anat Ben-David."

We were quiet for a moment. I leaned out of the way as one of the other waiters grabbed a tray of wineglasses from behind me. Then I employed my trademark interrogation technique. The one where I blurt out the first thing that comes to mind. "So, Anat, I have to say, it doesn't sound as if you like Yossi all that much."

She didn't seem particularly taken aback by my comment. "Maybe I liked him once, but now I don't care about him at all."

That certainly sounded familiar to me. I'd felt that way about plenty of guys. Like maybe twenty or so before I met Peter. "So, did you guys go out, or something?"

She blushed a little and busily rearranged the already perfectly arranged sushi plate. "Something like that. A long time ago, I liked him very much. And he pretended to like me. For maybe a week. And then nothing. Until I saw him again here in Los Angeles."

"With Fraydle," I said.

"With the Hasidic girl," Anat agreed.

Giving up on my shirt altogether, I stopped my ineffectual blotting and leaned on the counter. "Were they seeing each other for a long time?"

Anat handed the sushi plate to a waitress who was hovering nearby. "Months, I think. I used to see her in the building all the time. I don't think she's been there in the past week or two. At least, I haven't seen her. We have a courtyard, you know? Like on *Melrose Place*?"

I nodded.

"So, if she's been there when I've been there, I would see her. The last time I saw her she was very upset. "She was crying or something. She looked awful. Almost . . . not ugly, but just . . . I don't know . . . bad. Like something really terrible had happened to her."

"Did you talk to her?"

"Oh, no. I mean, I said hello sometimes, but she just

maybe nodded her head or something like that. She never talked to me. That last time she just ran by me."

"Do you think she knew about you and Yossi?"

"Maybe, but I don't think so. With Yossi, if he starts to talk about girlfriends, it would take a long time to finish the talk, you know?"

"Yeah, I've known guys like that. You know, you're probably lucky you only wasted a week of your life with him. Think how much worse it would be if you'd been with him for a year before you figured that out."

She smiled somewhat ruefully. "You know, you're right. I never thought of it that way."

"So, is there anything else you can tell me about Fraydle and Yossi?"

She pushed her hair out of her eyes with the back of her wrist. "I don't think so." At that moment, it seemed to dawn on her that she had no idea why I was asking her all these questions. "Are you a friend of hers?" she asked.

"No, not a friend," I replied. "Fraydle used to work for me. She's been missing for the past couple of days and I'm trying to help find her."

"Missing! Like she ran away or something?"

"Or something. Are you sure she hasn't been around Yossi's apartment?"

"I haven't seen her. But if we didn't come in at the same time, or if she just stayed in his apartment, I wouldn't necessarily know if she was there or not. I can give you our address. You can come over yourself and look." Anat picked up a pen and tore off a corner of a pastry box that was sitting on the table. She wrote out the address and handed it to me. "His apartment is on the bottom level, number four."

"Great, thanks, Anat. Here, take my phone number and call me if you think of anything or if you see her, okay?" I scrawled my name and number on another piece of the pastry box. She put it in her shirt pocket, said goodbye, and headed out of the kitchen holding the platter of raw fish.

As she walked out the kitchen door, Peter walked in. He looked relieved to see me.

"Hey! I've been looking all over for you. Are you okay? Did you get the stain out of your shirt?"

"I'm fine. My shirt is not so fine, however." I pulled at the fabric. It appeared that the milk had more or less rinsed out, but the fabric was bunched and crinkled where it had gotten wet. "Fabulous," I said forlornly.

"Oh, honey"—Peter crossed the room and took me in his arms—"you look beautiful. It doesn't matter if your shirt's a little wrinkled. Who cares? You're gorgeous."

I leaned into his chest and inhaled his familiar odor. Embracing him, I did my best not to cry. It had been a long time since Peter and I had just hugged each other. The combination of my postpartum moodiness and Peter's schedule had brought our relationship down to an unfamiliar low. It was hard to remember when we'd last had a conversation that didn't devolve into an argument.

Peter kissed the top of my head. "I love you, Juliet. You know that, don't you?"

"I know. I love you, too. I just seem to be soaking in some kind of perpetual hormonal bath. Ugh. The not sleeping isn't helping much, either."

"I'm so sorry, sweetie," he murmured. "I haven't been pulling my weight on that end, have I?"

I didn't answer. I didn't need to. I just buried my face a little deeper in his shirt.

"How about if I take baby duty two nights a week? I'll try to work it out on days when I don't have to be on the set, but I'll do it even if I have to work the next day. Okay?"

I leaned back and looked up at him. "That would be amazing, Peter. I think if I could get an uninterrupted six hours of sleep just two days in a row I would be in much better shape."

We smiled at each other.

"Look at the lovebirds hiding in the kitchen!" Maximum Mindy's voice rang out with a shrill falseness that was so obvious even Peter got it. He winced.

"Just a little breast-feeding accident," I said, glancing pointedly at her gravity-defying chest. "Let's go mingle, honey." I took Peter's hand and led him back out to the living room. Within a few minutes, I actually found someone with whom I enjoyed talking, another wife, this one married to an agent. She confided in me that she was ten weeks pregnant after three years of infertility treatments. By the end of the evening I knew all about her husband's low sperm motility and her endometriosis. We also talked for a while about her grandmother's recent Alzheimer's diagnosis and my two cesarean sections. Peter and the woman's husband discussed the Dodgers and their chances of winning the pennant.

It really is remarkable. Standing in line at a movie theater, I can learn more about a woman—her family, her academic background, and even her gynecological history—than my husband can learn about a man in five years of friendship. Women truly do share their lives with one another more easily than men. We confide and discuss, gossip and debate. I, for one, think that this willingness to let others in on our secrets is a source of our greatest strength. It is infinitely easier to survive a crisis, from a miscarriage to a husband's serious illness to a visit from your mother-in-law if you can turn to your friends, cry on their shoulders and gather energy, resources, and fortitude from their support. And, hey, if your friends aren't around, some woman you meet at a party can be almost as good.

It was almost eleven o'clock when Peter and I were ready to go. I hugged my new best friend, extended a warm if somewhat phony thanks to Miraculous Mindy, and went in search of Anat. I found her in the kitchen, washing dishes with another young woman in a caterer's jacket.

"Anat," I said. She turned to look at me. "We're heading home," I continued. "You have my number in case anything comes up."

"I have it," she replied. "Bye."

"Bye." As I was heading out the door I heard the second girl murmur something in Hebrew. Anat shrugged her shoulders in reply.

When Peter and I got home we found Ruby and Isaac asleep in their respective beds and Angelika lying stretched out on the couch. She jumped up when we came in.

"How were they?" I asked.

"Great! Really great," she answered. "Ruby's a doll. She worked on her project for the longest time and then she helped clean up everything without my even asking. She took a bath and didn't cry when I washed her hair. The baby slept for most of the evening, although he was up for the last hour or so. He crashed just about ten minutes ago."

Peter turned around and started walking back down the stairs.

"Hey!" I called. "Where are you going?"

"Home," he answered. "This is not our house."

"So, Angelika, what are you doing for the next, oh, eighteen years?" I asked.

I pressed some money into the girl's hand, over her strenuous objections. The only way I got her to accept it was by insisting that if she didn't take money from us I would feel uncomfortable asking her to baby-sit again. Peter walked her to her car and when he came back into the house, he found me lying in our bed. I'd somehow managed to cram myself into a black satin teddy he'd bought me as an anniversary present the year after we'd had Ruby. He crossed the room in about two steps and scooped me up in his arms. Then, we did something we hadn't done more than a couple of times since Isaac was born. And it was wonderful. Maybe, I thought, things were getting back to normal.

Ten

INSPIRED by my invigorating night, I decided that Isaac and I were going to get back into shape. I dressed him in his cutest outfit, a blue velour number with a purple collar and matching purple socks. I dressed myself in a less cute pair of leggings and a huge, ancient T-shirt of Peter's that said "Starfleet Academy" on the front and "Cadet" on the back. After dropping Ruby off at school, Isaac and I drove to Santa Monica to Yoga on Montana, the yoga studio where I'd done prenatal yoga during my pregnancy. I've always enjoyed yoga, particularly the position called *savasana*, which consists of lying on your back on the floor without moving, and I'd really meant to start doing it again as soon as the baby was born. The road to Weight Watchers is paved with good intentions.

I pulled into the parking lot and squeezed my Volvo station wagon in between a Mercedes wagon and a Land

Rover. The Mercedes had a child's car seat in the back and a bumper sticker that read "My Child Made the Honor Roll at the Oakville School." The Land Rover sported a bumper sticker with the slogan "My Kid Beat Up Your Honor Student." In Los Angeles people sometimes just let their cars do their fighting for them.

I walked into the class with Isaac balanced on my hip. He stared around the room, which was filled with other babies and their mothers. His eyes widened and he began to giggle. I wasn't sure what exactly had tickled his fancy, but I didn't care. I was just relieved that we seemed to be getting off to a good start. Maybe we could do this exercise thing after all. Grabbing a yoga mat for myself and a blanket for Isaac, I found myself a place on the floor. I rolled one end of the blanket and propped Isaac up on the roll. He smiled at me and I smiled back. Then I looked around the room. All the good cheer drained out of me as I realized the truth. I was a hippo in a herd of gazelles.

Yoga on Montana is very popular with the Hollywood crowd. The classes are usually chock-full of actresses, agents, and studio executives. Looking good is a primary occupation for these women, so, unsurprisingly, each and every member of my parental class had looked like a toothpick with an olive stuck on it. Now it was obvious that they'd all managed to get back to their pre-pregnancy weight before they'd even left the hospital.

I tucked my stomach in and tried to refrain from doing a self-hating body-fat comparison with every woman in the room. It was a challenge. And I failed. But who can blame me? As soon as I sat down I heard a minuscule blonde a few mats down from me say, "My trainer measured the circumference of my thighs the day I told him I was pregnant. It was sixteen inches. We remeasured every week throughout my pregnancy, and if it went up at all, we modified my workout regime and carb intake to deal with it." She gave her perfectly dyed hair a toss and patted her perfectly flat, lycra-enclosed belly. Her baby, also blond and about two months old, chose that moment to belch. At least I knew someone in that family was human.

A gamine-faced redhead with a made-over nose sitting next to the blonde squealed, "What a totally awesome idea! I can't believe I didn't think to do that! What was your final measurement?"

The blonde looked confused. "Final? What do you mean final? I told you. We never allowed it to increase."

At this point I glanced down at my legs. My ankles had a circumference of sixteen inches. I moved a little so that my legs were out of the stick figures' line of sight.

A third woman, wearing a leotard and tights in an acid green that perfectly matched both her headband and her son's jumpsuit, leaned over excitedly. "My secret was to have a nutritionist work with our cook so that every morsel that passed my lips was carefully vetted for fat and caloric content. I'm still doing it. Before we go out to eat, I have the restaurant fax the nutritionist a menu so that she can decide what I'm going to order. It's been working out so well. I only gained fourteen pounds in my entire pregnancy and I lost that within two weeks!"

The two others positively cooed in admiration.

I was just about ready to gather up my baby and head for the nearest Dunkin' Donuts when the instructor walked into the room. Valerie was actually a human being, with a stomach and legs instead of the washboard and pencils that were de rigueur in her classes. She was certainly not fat, but her body had a heft to it. Her muscles were strong and obvious and her belly looked round and soft. She was incredibly sexy, although I was sure that the other women in the class probably couldn't see that, since their ideal of physical attractiveness hovered somewhere between Kate Moss and Bergen-Belsen.

"Hello, ladies; hello, babies. Let's start with a meditation."

Isaac and I had a terrific time, despite my generalized misanthropy and tremendous feelings of insecurity. I did my Downward Dog and Warrior Stance with a flexibility that surprised the heck out of me. Isaac stared happily around and chewed on his blanket. At one point, Valerie picked him up and perched him on a big rubber ball, gently bouncing him up and down. About twenty minutes into the class I managed to forget about the way I looked and just enjoy the feeling of having my body move again. My muscles felt sore and kind of achy, but in a good way.

After the class was over, I picked up an oversized Smoothie made with blueberries and bananas and loaded Isaac into the car. I backed out of my parking space, missing the Mercedes in the next spot by a rather terrifying half an inch, and pulled onto Montana and headed for home. I'd been driving about five minutes when I began thinking about Fraydle again. Keeping my eyes on the road, or trying to, I groped in my bag for my cell phone. I spent a frustrating minute trying to remember what number I'd entered for Al Hockey on my speed-dial. I had no idea, but decided to take a stab at number 3. It seemed as likely as any other number. I got my mother instead.

"Hello?"

"Mom? Damn it."

"Juliet? What damn it?" she said, obviously a little confused about why her daughter would be calling and swearing at her.

"Nothing. I just meant to dial another number. I got you by accident."

"Of course. Why should you ever call your mother on purpose, God forbid?" Were we really having this conversation or was this a scene from a Woody Allen movie? My mother and I have always had a complicated relationship. We spend almost as much time talking to each other as we spend complaining about each other. I hold her responsible for all my various neuroses, and she holds herself responsible for all my good qualities. We fight constantly, but that never seems to keep us from being completely and totally wrapped up in one another's lives. I've been known to call her from a department store to describe an outfit so that she can weigh in on whether I should buy it. I never take her advice.

"Oh, Mom. Please. I call you all the time."

"When? When do you call me?"

"Yesterday! I talked to you yesterday."

"Yesterday? I called *you* yesterday. You did not call me."

"Oh what difference does that make? I talked to you yesterday. Anyway, Ma, I've got to go. I have to talk to Al Hockey."

"That nice man you used to work with? Why? Are you going back to work?" She sounded excited. No one had been more surprised than my mother when I'd quit work to stay home with my kids. For months she treated me to long, tearful conversations about my betrayal of everything she and her fellow bra-burners had suffered in order to make it possible for me to have the opportunities that I was throwing away so blithely. She reminded me of how she had always wanted to be a lawyer and had had to satisfy herself with a career as a legal secretary because she'd married so young and had to work to put my dad through school. She wept about my lost chance to make it to the United States Supreme Court.

"No. I'm not going back to work. Al is just helping me out with something."

"Helping you? With what? Oh, darling. Tell me you're not trying to get yourself shot again!" In the wake of the rather terrifying end to my last experience with private detection my mother had made me swear never to do anything like that as long as *she* lived.

"Give me a break, Ma. Okay? I'm not trying to get shot. I never tried to get shot to begin with. My baby-sitter ran away from home and Al is helping me find her. That's all."

"Your baby-sitter? Who knew you had a baby-sitter? I didn't, that's for sure. Why'd she run away?"

"I have no idea. Anyway, I have to go. I've got to call Al."

"When are we going to see you, Juliet? I wish we could come to California, but we can't leave Bubba."

"How is she?"

"Not so great. I don't think she's going to last long, honey. You should visit soon."

"I'm going to get there. I promise." I wasn't so sure that my grandmother wouldn't, in fact, live forever. She'd turned ninety-five the year before and gave no signs of throwing in the towel any time soon. "It's just a bad time for us, what with Peter's TV pilot. He's working all the time nowadays. There's just no way he can take the time off."

"So, *you* come. You come and bring my babies with you. It'll be a vacation for you. Daddy and I will take care of them, and you'll just relax. What could be better?"

"I'll think about it, Ma. Okay? I've really got to go."

"Okay, darling. I'll talk to you tomorrow."

I hung up the phone and sighed. I knew I should visit my grandmother. And it would be lovely to have my mother help me with the kids. I'd been pretty disappointed when she'd decided that she couldn't leave Bubba to come stay with us after Isaac was born. When I'd had Ruby, my mother had taken a leave of absence from her job and showed up in our apartment within hours of the birth. She cooked and cleaned for us for a solid month. It had been bliss and I'd really missed her this time around.

I gave up on my pathetic attempts to remember Al's number and called Directory Assistance. What is it about motherhood that causes women to get so dense? I used to be one of those organized people who could remember names, numbers, and even the occasional birthday. Now I was the kind of person who answered the door naked. It was as if every contraction had killed off a few hundred thousand brain cells. By the time both babies were out, I was left with the IQ of a ficus.

Al was out of the office when I called, but the receptionist put me through to his cell phone.

"Hey, Detective!" he greeted me.

"Cute. So, anything?"

"Nope. Nothing. One Jane Doe turned up in the past three days, but she's middle-aged and African-American. Not yours, I take it."

"Not mine. Mine's young and white."

"So you said. Anyway, I told my old sergeant to keep me posted if he hears anything. What else can I do for you?"

"Nothing right now, Al, but I might be calling you soon."

"I'll be expecting it."

At that moment I pulled into the intersection of Beverly Boulevard and Santa Monica. Home was to the right, but I continued straight and turned onto Melrose. I had an hour before I had to pick up Ruby. Just enough time to check out

Yossi's apartment. Maybe I'd luck out and find Fraydle
there.

I cruised down Melrose Avenue and started looking for a
parking space as soon as I saw Anat and Yossi's building.
After a frustrating few minutes, I pulled into the parking
lot of a Baby Gap. I slipped on Isaac's Baby Bjorn and, after scraping off some mysterious yellow gunk that had
managed to adhere itself to the front, strapped him into it
facing outward. He immediately began fussing, so I
slipped my pinky into his mouth. Sucking vigorously, he
quieted down. I walked briskly by the sign informing me
that cars belonging to those other than Gap customers
would be promptly towed. I was about to head down Melrose Avenue when I heard a terrifying trumpeting sound.

"Isaac! Are you kidding?" I pulled my smelly son out of
his Baby Bjorn and held him at arm's length. The little
wretch had managed to burst through his diaper yet again.
I looked back at the car. I'd remembered Barney tapes. I'd
remembered diapers. I'd remembered wipes. I'd even
brought the Baby Bjorn. But I'd forgotten a spare outfit.
Once again, my place in the pantheon of bad mothers was
assured.

Still holding Isaac out in front of me, I hustled into the
Baby Gap and was immediately greeted by a smiling Gen-
Xer. I responded to her "Hi! How are you?" with a wave of
my malodorous child. She pointed to someone whose job
actually consisted of helping people and not just welcom-
ing them. I balanced Isaac precariously on my hip, trying
to touch as little of his body as possible, reached into my
purse, and tossed my credit card at the salesclerk.

"What can I get for you?" she asked.

"Something clean," I said.

She directed me to a bathroom where I stripped the baby down and washed him in the sink. I looked at what had once been my favorite baby outfit, now stained a horrifying shade of yellow, and debated throwing it out. I couldn't bring myself to part with it, so I shoved it into a sanitary napkin disposal bag and hid that in the bottom of my diaper bag.

Isaac and I found our salesclerk standing at the register holding a miniature pair of jeans, a rugby shirt, and matching socks. I dressed the baby, using my teeth to tear the price tags off. I handed the damp pieces of paper back to the be-pierced salesclerk, who gingerly scanned them into the register. We were in and out in less than five minutes. And we managed to spend less than seventy dollars. A miracle.

From the outside, the building where I hoped to find Fraydle hiding out was fairly nondescript. It was Spanish-style in the way that most Los Angeles houses of the 1930s are, that is to say it was stucco with wrought-iron railings. The façade was thickly covered in ivy that had been inelegantly hacked away from the windows. The entry was through an archway whose stone-faced interior walls were covered in brightly colored graffiti, some of it in Hebrew.

Isaac and I passed under the arch and into a courtyard. Once, it must have been beautiful. A stone fountain dominated the center of the yard. In its large oval pond, a mermaid balanced on her tail, her face raised to the sky. Her nose was chipped off, and there was a rusted pipe poking out of the top of her head. At one time water probably cascaded down in a lovely mist. Now, the bone-dry pond was filled with cigarette butts and the odd beer bottle.

The ground-floor apartments opened out into the courtyard, two on each side. The tenants of each of the eight apartments were obviously responsible for taking care of the area immediately in front of their front doors. One had decorated carefully, with colorful flowers growing in large tubs and a pair of Adirondack chairs. Most of the others had at least a folding lawn chair or two. One or two were barren of porch accessories.

In the back corner of the courtyard, I noticed a flight of stairs leading up to the second-floor apartments. These were accessible by a long exterior hallway, like a wraparound porch, that circled the second floor.

Number 4 had in front of it a pair of beat-up lounge chairs with webbing that might have once been red but had faded to a rusty pink. There was a green window box propped against the wall next to the door and a tomato plant climbed out of the box and up the wall. I glanced down at Isaac. He had spat out my finger and was busily sucking on the folded front of his Baby Bjorn. I kissed the top of his head and knocked on the door to Yossi's apartment.

Within moments the door opened. Yossi stood there wearing only a pair of low-slung jeans. His bare chest was covered with a thatch of black hair that thinned down to a line as it crept down his flat stomach into the top of his pants. The button of his jeans was undone. It was everything I could do not to stare at him. It had been a while since I'd seen a bared twenty-something chest in the flesh. I looked up into his blue eyes. He didn't look particularly happy to see me.

"Hi," I said.

"She is not here."

"But she's been here before."

He looked me up and down for a minute. I hadn't bothered to change after yoga so I was still wearing nothing but a pair of leggings and a T-shirt. "You are a friend of Fraydle's parents?" he asked, sounding doubtful.

"She worked for me. I told you that at Nomi's, remember?"

"You are not Orthodox?"

I laughed. "Do I look Orthodox to you?"

He looked me up and down again, reading my T-shirt carefully as if trying to decide whether the Starfleet Academy was the flagship of a brand new chain of yeshivas. "Today, not so much. But at Nomi's you did."

"What are you talking about?" I tried to remember what I'd worn to the Israeli restaurant. And then I realized. A long black skirt, long-sleeved white shirt, and, most damningly, a beret to hide my hair. Of course he'd thought I was Orthodox. As soon as he'd seen me, Yossi had probably assumed I was a friend of Fraydle's parents or, at the very least, a member of her community. No wonder he wouldn't talk to me.

"Yossi. We need to talk. I'm not one of Fraydle's parents' friends. I'm not Orthodox. I'm just a woman that Fraydle worked for once who is worried about her. Just like I'm sure you are. She's missing and if there is anything you know that can help me to find her, you need to tell me. Her parents and aunt are out of their minds with worry."

He leaned against the door to his apartment for a moment and then, shutting it carefully behind him, sat down in one of the lounge chairs. He motioned me to sit in the other. I perched carefully on the edge, bouncing Isaac gently. I was afraid that if Isaac sensed I had actually gotten off my feet, he would start fussing. Miraculously, he seemed not to notice.

"Is Fraydle here, Yossi?"

He leaned back against his chair with a sigh and said, "No. She is not here. She is not with me. I wish she was with me. I asked her to come with me many times. But she always says no. Deep in her heart, Fraydle is a good girl. She does what her father tells her to do." This last part was said with bitterness.

"Yossi," I said, "was Fraydle your girlfriend?"

He scowled. "Can she be my girlfriend if she is not allowed to see me? Can she be my girlfriend if we never spend more than an hour or two together?"

"I don't know. Can she? Listen, Yossi, I know she left here very upset not long ago. What happened?"

He didn't answer.

"Tell me, exactly what are you and Fraydle to each other?"

He didn't answer.

"I know that you don't think this is any of my business, but maybe we can work together to figure out where Fraydle has gone."

He remained silent.

"Is it that you're afraid I'll tell her parents about you two? Is that it?"

Silence.

Finally, Yossi sighed. "It doesn't matter now." He took a deep breath as if to fortify himself for the story he was about to tell. Then he began: "Fraydle and I met about nine or ten months ago. I came to her aunt's store on my third day in Los Angeles. I was staying with an old friend of my mother's. This woman asked me to shop for her in the kosher grocery stores, so I came in with a long list and Fraydle helped me. She found everything on the list and even helped me to carry the bags and boxes to the bus stop.

And she talked to me. Just for a minute. But she was so beautiful. Her eyes. You know how beautiful she is."

"Yes, her eyes really are quite remarkable. Violet, like Liz Taylor's," I said.

"Who?"

"Elizabeth Taylor? The movie actress?"

He shook his head.

"Okay, whatever—you met, you talked. And then?"

"And then not so much for a while. I came to the store every day, every two days. Sometimes she helped me. Sometimes she stayed in the back and her aunt helped me. And then, one day, I came to the shop and she was not there at all. I came only to see her, I needed nothing. I bought a chocolate bar just to buy something and I went to the bus stop to wait for my bus. Fraydle was sitting on the bench waiting also for the bus.

"At first I thought it was only a coincidence that we met, but she told me later that she waited for me. I sat down next to her and we talked. All the time we talked, she looked around to make sure nobody noticed that we were together. When the bus came, we got on. I sat down in a seat and she sat in the seat in front of me, not next to me, so no one would think we were together. We rode around the entire city. For two hours we rode the bus, talking and talking. She told me about her family, about the books she read. I told her about my family, about my military service, about Israel. We just talked. Finally, the bus made a full circle and we were back on Melrose and La Brea. We made a date to see each other again on the bus.

"For two months, that is all we did. Three, maybe four times a week we would see each other. I would get on the bus by the house where I was staying, and she would get

on at her corner. We would ride for one full circle. Sometimes she had one of her baby brothers or sister with her.
She would hold the baby and we would talk and ride the
bus. Once or twice people got on with her, people from
her synagogue or other Hasidim from the neighborhood.
We always sat in different rows, so when that happened
we just pretended to be strangers.

"After a while, we started getting off the bus in different
parts of the city. We went to the La Brea Tar Pits. We went
to the Los Angeles County Museum of Art. We went to
cafés."

I interrupted him. "She ate at non-kosher restaurants
with you?"

"No, never. She drank only water or tea. Once, she
sipped my latte. She never ate."

"And that's all you did, Yossi? Ride the bus and tour Los
Angeles?"

"For a long time, yes. And then I got a job. I work as a
security guard. It's nights and weekends, mostly, but sometimes I have to work during the day. We saw each other
less and less. One week, we missed altogether. That was
very bad."

"So what did you do?"

He swallowed nervously and paused for a moment as if
to decide whether or not to continue his story.

"I got this apartment. I took it because it was near her
house. She would come here when she could get away,
sometimes early in the morning, sometimes in the afternoon. I never knew when she would come, and sometimes
I was at work so I missed her. But still, we met a few times
every week."

"It's a little unusual for a Hasidic girl to meet a man at
his apartment, don't you think?" I asked.

"We are in love!" he said. "I love her. She loves me. It is not like what you think."

"No, I'm sure it's not. I'm sorry," I said soothingly. "So when was the last time you saw her?"

He sighed. "A few weeks ago she came here, as usual, but afterwards she told me it was the last time. She told me that her parents had found a *shiddach*, a match, for her and that she'd accepted him.

"I knew they were bringing men to her. Each time before she rejected them. But this time, she said yes. I begged her, please marry me. I begged her, come with me back to Israel. She said no. She said she had to do what her father told her. Fraydle is always a good girl." He rubbed his eyes angrily. "So, that is our story. I saw her only once after that. I came looking for her at her aunt's store. I walked around the neighborhood, and I found her in the park with your baby. I asked her again to come with me. I showed her these." He reached into the front pocket of his jeans and pulled out a crumpled airline ticket folder. He handed it to me. Inside the folder were two TWA tickets to Israel. One was in the name of Yossi Zinger. The other read Fraydle Finkelstein. The flight had left at four o'clock the day before.

"All the money I saved these past months I spent on these tickets. You see, they are business class. Not coach."

I looked at the crumpled tickets. The tickets had cost $3,140.21. Each. "But she wouldn't go," I said.

"No. She said, 'I love you, Yossi.' But I know she loves her father more."

"Maybe she was afraid. She's a young girl; maybe the idea of leaving her home and her family was just too scary for her."

"Maybe. But she has left now, hasn't she? Where is she? Where is Fraydle?"

"I haven't any idea. Is there someone you can think of who might know? Did she have a friend, maybe someone outside her community to whom she would go?"

"Me. She had me."

"What happened the day she left here, crying?"

"What are you talking about?"

"One of your neighbors saw her leave your apartment in tears."

He looked intensely uncomfortable. "Nothing. Just . . . just a fight about her not wanting to come to Israel with me."

At that moment, Isaac began to howl. I stood up and started bouncing him up and down.

"Okay, honey. Just one more minute." I turned to Yossi. "Look, I have to go pick my daughter up at school and get this baby to bed. But we need to talk more. Is there a number where I can reach you?"

"You can call me on my cell phone," he said. Ah, L.A., where even illegal-alien security guards have wireless connections. I paced back and forth with my crying baby while Yossi went inside for a piece of paper and a pen to write down his number. I crammed the scrap into my purse and, with a quick goodbye, hustled out of the building.

Eleven

I arrived at Beth El Nursery School to find Ruby sitting in the time-out chair. Brenda, my favorite of Ruby's teachers, was hovering around her, obviously at a loss. Ruby's arms were crossed over her chest, her shoulders were raised up to her ears, and she was scowling so hard her cheeks had turned white. Business as usual.

"Hey, Ruby. Hi, Brenda. What's up?" I was doing my best to come across as upbeat and cheerful, with just a touch of concern. I probably sounded just like I felt: embarrassed and wondering whether anyone would mind if I chose this moment to throttle my kid.

"Hello, Juliet. Ruby's having a hard time this afternoon." I'd never heard Brenda sound anything but sweet before. I'd never even known irritation was part of her repertoire.

"It sure looks that way," I said. "What happened?"

"Honestly, I wish I knew. She had to spend two minutes in the time-out chair because she bit Alexander, but that was half an hour ago. She's refused to get up."

"You bit Alexander!" I said, crouching down to Ruby's level. "What were you thinking? You know biting is a bad thing to do." I looked up at Brenda. "This really isn't like her. She's not a biter."

Brenda just smiled thinly.

"Ruby! Talk to me!" I said. "What's going on here?"

My daughter looked up at me, her grim little face screwed up in outrage. Clearly, it was too much that her mother had joined her oppressors. Tears gathered in her eyes and spilled over onto her cheeks. She collapsed into my arms with a wail. I stroked her back and murmured, "Okay, honey. Okay. It's all right. It's over now. Tell Mama what happened."

"It's not fair!" she sobbed. "Brenda is mean!"

"Brenda is not mean, Ruby. She's nice. You like Brenda. She put you in the time-out chair because you did a bad thing, not because she's mean. But kiddo, you could have been out long ago. You're the one who chose to sit here all afternoon."

She looked up at me. "Alex bited me first! I just bited him back. But Brenda didn't see him bite me. She only saw me bite him. But I bited him *back*. I told Brenda that I'm not getting up until she says she's sorry for giving me a time-out and not Alex."

That's my kid for you. Willing to ruin her own fun just to prove a point. Well, for all her sweetness, Brenda was too firm to give into the convoluted sense of justice of a three-year-old. But neither did I intend to spend the day, week, or month indulging this sit-down strike.

"Here's the thing, Ruby. Brenda didn't do anything

wrong. She's not going to apologize. I'm going to get your lunchbox, and then Isaac and I are going to go home, get the stroller, and walk to the store to get a chocolate bar. You can either come with us, or stay here all day."

Ruby struggled for a moment, but finally gave in, as I knew she would.

By the time we'd reached our house Ruby had bargained her way into two chocolate bars and a bag of *gelt*. It remains a mystery to me how a person who could negotiate effectively with the nastiest and most powerful of federal prosecutors could fall entirely apart when faced with a wily three-year-old. It all probably comes down to the fact that I'd never gone into a negotiation on behalf of a client feeling bad because it had been weeks since I'd taken the prosecutor to the park or played Candyland with him. Guilt is a powerful thing.

When we wheeled our way into the kosher grocery, we found Nettie seated on a high stool behind the counter, leaning wearily on her elbows. Her face was crumpled and her wig looked uncombed. She'd aged years since the afternoon she'd first suggested that Fraydle work for me. When we came in, she roused herself to smile at Ruby and pat her red curls, but then sighed again. Isaac had fallen asleep in the stroller on the walk over to the store, so, once I'd hushed Ruby with her candy bars, Nettie and I were able to talk in peace.

"No news," I said, rather than asked.

"Nothing."

"Nettie, it's been three days. It's time to do something about this."

"I know. I know. I've been saying this to Baruch from the beginning. He must get help from outside. He must call the police."

"But he won't."

"No." She rubbed her brow.

"Nettie. You must see how this looks. It looks like he isn't interested in finding her. If he really cared, he would call the police!"

She shook her head. "You don't understand. Baruch is dying inside, I'm telling you. He does nothing but look for his child. But we are not like you. We have our own ways. We help ourselves."

"But clearly your ways aren't working! You haven't found her yet. And every day that passes makes it less likely that you will."

"I tell my brother every day, please call the police. But he won't. He is a stubborn man, Mrs. Applebaum. He is a stubborn man."

"What about Mrs. Finkelstein?" I asked. "Do you think she might be willing to talk to the police? Just to report Fraydle missing?"

"I don't know. I don't think so."

"Well, have you talked to her about it? Have you suggested calling the police?"

Nettie leaned over the counter and grabbed my hand. "You do it!" she said. "You talk to her. Maybe she'll listen to you."

I disengaged from her hot, dry grasp. "Nettie, your brother won't even talk to me on the phone. He's certainly not going to let me into his house."

"He's not home!" she said. "He's out looking for Fraydle. He's out driving night and day. You go now, you'll find just Sima, my sister-in-law. Go now! It will take you only a moment. I'll watch your children."

I looked at her doubtfully for a moment. But the truth

was, I felt guilty. I hadn't told Fraydle's parents about Yossi, and I wasn't planning to. The least I could do was try to convince them to report their daughter's disappearance to the police.

"Okay." I agreed. I checked on Isaac, who was still sleeping and told Ruby I'd be right back. She opened her mouth to protest, but snapped it shut and smiled at Nettie, who was dangling a little mesh bag of gold coins in front of her eyes.

"Oooh. *Gelt*," Ruby breathed.

"You like chocolate, *maydele*?" Nettie said, unwrapping one and handing it to Ruby. Ruby crammed it in her mouth and held her hand out for another. "One at a time, darling." Nettie stroked her hair and cupped a palm on her cheek. She turned to me. "So go already," she said.

I left the store by the back door and walked over to Fraydle's house. I opened the creaky little gate and found two little boys around Ruby's age or a bit younger playing at the top of the long flight of steps leading to the front porch. Their mouths opened in round O's as I came up the stairs. One of them, the older, shouted something in Yiddish and ran inside the house. The younger popped his thumb in his mouth and sucked it, all the while backing carefully away from me. I smiled at him, but his eyes just grew bigger and he moved a little more quickly.

I reached the front door just as Sima Finkelstein walked through the doorway. She was holding a dishtowel in one hand and another little boy on her hip. Her long skirt was covered with a flowered apron.

"Yes?" she said.

"Hello, Mrs. Finkelstein. I'm Juliet Applebaum. I was here a couple of days ago?"

"Yes. Yes, of course. You have news about Fraydle? You know where she is?"

"No. No, I'm terribly sorry. I haven't found her. Could I come in for a moment?"

She hesitated, but then stepped back and motioned me through the door. I walked quickly into the house and back to the kitchen. She followed me. There was a baby asleep in a bouncy seat on the kitchen counter and Sarah, Fraydle's sister, stood at the sink washing dishes. She looked up when I walked in the room, but blushed and looked down again when I said hello.

Sima motioned me to a chair. She set the little boy down on the floor and he toddled off. She sat down next to me. "Can I get you something? A glass of tea?" she asked.

"That would be lovely."

"Sarahleh. Put the kettle on for tea."

The girl obeyed, filling the dented metal teakettle from the sink.

Suddenly, there was a crash of crockery. The shock of the noise made me jump in my chair. The baby woke with a cry and Sima stood up and rocked the bouncy seat. Sarah stood at the sink, stock-still.

"Sarahleh, what happened? Did you break something?" her mother asked.

"No, no. I just dropped a plate. It's fine. See?" The girl held up a blue saucer with small white flowers. Her mother nodded and sat down again. The baby stopped her cries and settled down. Sima closed her eyes, as if exhausted. I looked over to Sarah in time to see her surreptitiously slipping the broken pieces of what looked like another saucer into the pocket of her skirt. When the girl realized that I had seen her, her face turned ashen and she looked at me, wide-eyed. I smiled in what I hoped was a reassuring way.

She took a breath and turned back to the sink. I shook my head at the thought of a house where the consequences of breaking a plate were so terrifying.

I turned back to the girl's mother. "Mrs. Finkelstein, I'll be perfectly honest with you. I came here to try to convince you to report Fraydle's disappearance to the police."

Sima shook her head. "That is my husband's decision, Mrs. Applebaum. He will decide if that is appropriate. For now, we are looking for her ourselves."

"I understand that, Mrs. Finkelstein. But I also know that the longer you wait, the harder it will be for the police to find Fraydle once you do go to them. The trail will be colder. Do you understand what I mean?"

The woman nodded her head slightly and stared down at her hands. They were work-roughened and red and the nails were bitten almost to the quick. Her cuticles were torn and chewed. She grasped her right hand with her left, twisting her wedding ring.

"Mrs. Finkelstein. Sima," I said, "please, we must do something here. What if she hasn't run off? What if something really happened to her? Every minute you wait makes it less and less likely that you'll find her."

The rabbi's wife looked up at me, gathered herself together, and spoke. "I know you are trying to help. But this is not your business. My husband will find Fraydle. He does not need the police or any of you to help him." She rose from her chair and walked out of the kitchen. Grudgingly, I followed her. I walked out the front door that she held open for me, down the steps, and out the gate.

This family, these people, were a mystery to me. Like my own grandparents, theirs had probably come to America from a *shtetl*, a tiny, Jewish village in Eastern Europe. The isolationist life steeped in tradition and religious observance that Fraydle's family led in the heart of Los Angeles was not much different than the lives led by our respective great-grandparents in Poland, Lithuania, or Russia. My assimilated life, with my non-Jewish husband, was two or three or ten worlds apart. How was it that people from the same place, brought up in the same religion, ended up so entirely different?

I trudged back to Nettie's store and found her crouched on the floor, blowing soap bubbles for Isaac, whom she'd propped up into a sitting position. He was giggling hysterically as Ruby chased the bubbles around the store. The few customers who'd arrived in my absence did not seem to mind having to wait to make their purchases. All of them older women, they leaned against the counter and smiled at my children.

When Nettie noticed me, she hoisted herself up off the floor with a groan and busied herself checking out the line of waiting women. When they'd all left, she turned to me.

"And? What did she say?"

"She refused to consider it. She said her husband knows best."

Nettie snorted derisively.

"Nettie, tell me about this match of Fraydle's."

"The Hirsch boy? A wonderful match for Fraydle. An important family. And wealthy."

"Yes, you told me that. Did Fraydle agree to the match?"

"Everyone agreed. Baruch is thrilled. The Hirsch family is happy. The boy likes her. It's all set."

"And Fraydle's mother? What does she think?"

"Ah, Sima." Nettie shook her head. "Sima wants Fraydle to choose for herself. Sima is a big believer in love matches. Don't ask me why; hers certainly wasn't one. Her parents chose for her and that was that. And Sima and

Baruch have been very happy. Happy enough. Anyway, they have a lovely family."

"Did Fraydle choose what's-his-name, Hirsch?"

Nettie looked uncomfortable. "Ari Hirsch. The boy's name is Aharon, but they call him Ari."

"Did she choose Ari Hirsch for herself?" I was getting insistent.

"Not specifically," Nettie replied.

"What does that mean? Not specifically? Did she say she would marry him or not?"

Nettie shrugged her shoulders. "She didn't agree, not exactly. But she didn't reject him, either. She told Baruch she needed more time. She said she would do as her parents asked and marry, but she needed more time to decide if she wanted to marry Ari Hirsch."

A thought occurred to me. If this marriage was so important to her father, and if she had refused to obey him, would he, could he, have tried to force her?

"Nettie, I have a question for you. I don't want you to take this the wrong way, but what would your brother have done if Fraydle refused to marry the boy? Would he have made her do it, anyway?"

Nettie looked at me. She shook her head firmly. "Baruch, maybe he would have tried to make Fraydle marry Ari Hirsch, but Sima wouldn't stand for it. I told you, she always insisted that the girl be allowed to make a free choice. She would never have let my brother force a match on her daughter."

A possibility was beginning to occur to me.

"But let's say somehow Rabbi Finkelstein got Fraydle to do it. Would Sima object to the marriage once it had happened?"

"A marriage is a marriage. Once it's done, that's it."

"Look, Nettie, there's got to be a reason your brother is refusing to get the police involved in the disappearance of his child. Maybe he's unwilling because he knows where she is. Is it possible that your brother sent Fraydle to the Hirsches, maybe against her wishes, and without Sima knowing about it?"

Nettie looked at me. To my surprise, she did not seem at all shocked at my question. "Anything is possible," she said.

Twelve

BY the time Peter walked in the door at ten o'clock that night, I'd already decided what I was going to do. He came into the bedroom and found me standing over Isaac's changing table, which we'd moved into our room once we'd realized he wasn't going to be sleeping in his and Ruby's room any time soon. I was holding my nose and dabbing at the mess in front of me.

"Hey, honey," Peter said, kissing me on the cheek. "That's gross."

"I know. Totally disgusting," I agreed. "Why is it *green*? I swear this kid did not eat anything today that was this particular shade of fluorescent green."

"Here, you take a break, I'll deal with this."

I handed over the box of wipes and, after washing my hands, stretched out on the bed.

"Listen, Peter, my mom's been bugging me to go visit her and my dad in New Jersey."

"I can't possibly get away right now."

"No, I know that. I was thinking of just me and the kids."

"Okay."

And that was it. No *Please don't leave me*. No *I'll be lost without you*. Nothing.

When I told my mother that we'd decided to come out and visit, she positively crowed with delight. She inventoried all the baby items she needed to borrow or buy and almost hung up on me in her eagerness to get started setting up the kids' room. I managed to get plane tickets for the next redeye to New York. Thank God for frequent-flyer miles. I debated using another 25,000 miles to get Isaac a seat of his own but decided to risk having him on my lap. After all, how many people would be flying to New York in the middle of the night in the middle of the week? I packed three suitcases full of everything I could imagine ever needing, including a breast pump, ten changes of clothing for the kids, every infant medication known to humankind, and an assortment of toys, games, rattles, and dolls. You would have thought we were setting out for a year at the South Pole, rather than a week in Northern New Jersey, the shopping-center capital of the world.

The next evening, Peter drove us to the airport and insisted on parking and taking us to the gate, even though I'd offered to martyr myself at the curbside check-in. He schlepped my sixty pieces of carry-on luggage for me and entertained Ruby while I gave Isaac one last preflight diaper change. When the preboarding announcement came, he grabbed me and wrapped me in a bear hug.

"I'm going to miss you guys," he croaked, resting his face on the top of my head.

"We'll miss you, too." I reached up to kiss him, but Ruby wriggled in between us, forcing me to step back and out of his arms. He gave her a kiss goodbye and then transferred all the various bags to me. I walked down the ramp pushing Isaac in his folding stroller, holding Ruby's hand, with Isaac's car seat in the other hand, the diaper bag around my neck, a flight bag full of snacks and toys hanging from each shoulder, and my purse clenched in my teeth.

The flight was every bit as horrific as I'd expected, and then some. While it had certainly occurred to me that Isaac might spit up all over himself, I forgot that a goodly portion could land on me. I'd brought plenty of changes of clothing for him, but none for myself. By the time we got off the plane we were a sight to behold.

My parents swept us up in their arms and packed us into their massive Chrysler. We stopped at my grandmother's nursing home on the way to their house, and my parents entertained the kids in the solarium while I held my grandmother's hand. She didn't recognize me. My mother had prepared me for that, but it came as a shock nonetheless.

Once we got back in the car, I fell asleep immediately and barely woke up to walk into my parents' house and crawl up the stairs to my old room. Hours later, when I'd slept enough to recover from the flight, I ambled downstairs to find my children happily playing in the kitchen in which I'd grown up. The radio was, as usual, earsplittingly loud. My parents' radio is perpetually tuned, full blast, to a news station. Until I started spending time at friends' houses in grade school I'd assumed all families carried out conversations over the blare of a radio announcer yelling,

"You give us ten minutes, we'll give you the world."

I walked across the room and turned off the radio. I rubbed my eyes and smiled at my mother and father.

"What time is it?"

"Two in the afternoon," my father answered. His hair had grown even more Einstein-like in the months since I'd seen him. It stood up in soft white peaks all over his head. His blue eyes looked out of a crinkled face and his cheeks were slightly reddened. I kissed his bald spot.

"Hi, Daddy. I've missed you."

"We've missed you, too, *mamaleh*. Ruby here is teaching me how to color a rainbow." Ruby was perched on his lap, a red crayon gripped firmly in her hand. Next to my tiny girl, my father looked even older than his seventy-five years. Sometime in junior high school I realized that my parents were much older than those of my friends. My mother had me when she was forty, long after she'd given up hopes of having a child. My younger brother came along just two years later. Back then, before the dawn of the age of Pergonal and Chlomid, that was decidedly rare.

My parents came from a different generation than the other parents they saw at ballet recitals and Little League. Their Brooklyn accents and the *yiddishisms* peppering their speech gave them a vaguely Old World air. They cared more about politics and social justice and less about material acquisitions than most of the other grownups I knew. As an adult, I grew to be proud of them and glad to have been raised in a house where Woody Guthrie songs were sung at bedtime and a McGovern poster hung in our window well into the mid-seventies. As a child, I'm ashamed to admit that they embarrassed me.

I walked around the table to where my mother was sitting, holding Isaac. She was feeding him a bottle full of yellowish liquid. It gave me a moment's pang of concern. The only thing he'd consumed thus far in his life was breast milk.

"I'm giving the boy some chamomile tea," my mother said. "It says in that book over there that it's good for them." She pointed to a brightly colored tome on the kitchen table. I pulled it over and read the title: *The Holistic Baby*.

"Wow," I said.

"Listen, alternative medicine is a perfectly legitimate thing. Don't be so dismissive," she said. My mother has always been willing to jump on any new philosophical bandwagon, especially if the word "alternative" can be used to describe it. She was a beatnik, a hippie, an ardent feminist (that one stuck) and now, apparently, she was into the New Age. But she always looked exactly the same. Like a Jewish grandmother from Brooklyn.

"What dismissive?" I protested. "How am I being dismissive? I just said 'Wow.' "

"It was your tone."

"What tone? There was no tone."

"Ladies, ladies," my father interrupted. "Could we please have five minutes of peace and harmony before the fighting begins?" That's my father's job. Mom and I argue, and he steps in and referees.

"Mama and Grandma are fighting?" Ruby said, sitting bolt-upright on her grandfather's lap.

"Nobody's fighting," I said. And we really weren't. We were just bickering, like we always do.

"Hi, Ma." I kissed her on the cheek. She handed the baby over to me. He immediately began rooting around my shirt front, so I sat down and took out a breast to nurse. My father blushed and began closely studying Ruby's drawing.

"So, Ma, are you taking time off while we're here?" I asked.

"Of course," she said, nodding her head vigorously, the tight gray curls of her perm bouncing like so many little antennae. My mother's undying loyalty to the hairstyle she'd chosen in the mid-seventies is a source of mystery to me. Every three months she spends two hours in Hair-o-matic, having her steel-colored locks tightly wound up in pink rods. Because she's rail-thin and about four foot ten, she looks decidedly like a Q-tip. In fact, when I was in my senior year of high school, she greeted trick-or-treaters wearing a white tunic and tights, with her hair dusted in baby powder. I was the only one who got the joke. The other kids all thought she was supposed to be a nurse.

I popped Isaac off my nipple and propped him on my shoulder where he promptly let loose with a tremendous belch. My parents burst into a round of applause. You would have thought he'd just hit the winning run in the World Series.

"So, Ma, Daddy, do you know any Hasidic Jews in Borough Park? Preferably Verbover." I asked.

My father wrinkled his brow and tapped his chin with one finger. "Margie, didn't the son of one of your Russian cousins become a Hasid?" he asked my mother.

"What *tsuris* that family had. They weren't here six months before Anatole, the father, had to have bypass surgery. They were burned out of their first apartment, and the insurance company wouldn't pay off. Then, that terrible thing with the daughter's baby. It was born d-e-a-d."

"And the Hasidic son?" I reminded them, just in case they'd forgotten that I had actually asked for something other than a litany of familial tragedy.

"What was his name, Gene? Do you remember?" my mother asked.

"It was something Russian. And then he changed it to

Jewish. Like Sasha to Schmuel. Or Boris to Binyamin. Like that," my father answered.

I rolled my eyes. Getting a straight answer out of my parents was harder than getting Isaac to sleep through the night. I bounced the baby on my knee, trying not to express my impatience.

"I remember!" my mother shouted. "Josef. That's his name."

"What's Russian about that? Or Yiddish for that matter?" I asked.

"Nothing. Who knows where your father got that. He's senile. Ignore him."

"What senile? It's spelled with an *F*, that's Russian."

"This Russian Josef, do you think I could call him?" I asked.

"I don't see why not," my mother said. She picked up the phone and riffled through her ancient Museum of Modern Art address book. She found the number and dialed it on the telephone stuck to the wall next to the fridge. My mother's hair isn't the only seventies throwback in my parents' house. They don't own a cordless phone, but rather make do with a couple of ancient appliances that they used to rent from Bell Telephone. The one in the kitchen has an extra long cord that is still twisted in the knots I made while talking endlessly to my high school girlfriends about whether Larry Pitkowsky did, indeed, like me or if Maxine Fass was his dream girl. They also have a couple of old TVs, one of which has a pair of rusty pliers permanently attached to it in place of the channel dial. I think the dial got lost sometime when I was in elementary school. Back then the set only reliably received two channels, PBS and some religious station out of upstate New York. My mother used to insist that that was precisely enough TV. PBS gave us a little culture and the religious station allowed us to understand the true soul of America. Or something like that.

My mother mouthed "machine" at me and waited for a moment, then said, into the phone, "Josef, this is your cousin Margie. Margie Applebaum. Remember my daughter, Juliet? The one who went to Harvard Law School? She's in town and would love to talk to you. Give us a call." She left the number and hung up. There are an infinite number of ways to work the words "Harvard Law School" into a sentence, and my mother has mastered them all. I've heard her respond to an innocuous comment about the weather with a declamation on how her daughter had suffered through the bitter Cambridge winters while attending law school.

"Not home," she said.

"So I gathered," I replied.

I sat quietly for a while, sipping at the coffee my father had poured for me while my mother was on the phone. I could think of only one other Hasidic Jew who might be willing to give me a little insight into their community. She might even know the famous Hirsches of Borough Park.

Libby Bernstein nee Barret, my freshman-year roommate at Wesleyan University, was a daughter of a Daughter of the American Revolution and member of the Mayflower Association, who had somehow ended up an Orthodox Jew. Her husband, Josh Bernstein, was a couple of years ahead of us at college. They'd begun dating at the end of our freshman year. After he graduated, Josh moved to Brooklyn. He'd started out as a run-of-the-mill, assimilated Jewish kid, but as he got older he become more and more interested in religious Judaism. After graduation, he joined the Verbover Hasidic community. After a while Josh must have realized that he couldn't be an Orthodox Jew and date a *shiksa*. He broke up with Libby, and she was utterly devastated. She spent two weeks crying on the shoulder of every one of her friends, me included, and then took off for Brooklyn herself. She begged Josh to take her back and promised she would do whatever it took to be with him.

Libby never came back to college. She moved in with a Hasidic family and began to study for conversion. Her host family had nine children; Libby was an only child from a WASPy New England family. The contrast between her silent home and the apartment stuffed with children must have been astonishing. Libby's mother had died when she was in high school and the woman of the house became a second mother to her. I know Libby had longed for a mother-daughter relationship, and I'm sure it felt wonderful to have a woman take care of her, and teach her.

When I'd call Libby on the phone from college she would wax rhapsodic about Yaffa, her "mother." She told me they spent hour after hour in the kitchen, drinking tea, cooking, talking. There was an endless amount of work to do in that house, what with all the children, but Libby said Yaffa never seemed overwhelmed. Every day had its schedule, its activities, and Libby and Yaffa did them together. Yaffa would quiz Libby on her Hebrew and on Bible studies while they kneaded dough or chopped onions.

Libby's conversion was complete within two years, and, with the Verbover *rebbe*'s permission, she and Josh married in a traditional ceremony. It was kind of a trip for the few of us who came down from Wesleyan for it. We women were kept strictly separate from the men. We sat by ourselves, ate by ourselves, and even danced by ourselves. But it was pretty incredible. People were so full of joy, whirling and twirling to the *klezmer* band. And Libby seemed genuinely delighted with the life she'd chosen. I remember dancing the hora at the wedding, feeling as if I were part of something ancient, exciting, and beautiful. People, my people, had danced to this music for hundreds of years. It was so compelling and wonderful that it made someone like Libby desperate to be a part of it, of us. When Peter and I were married people danced the hora; they even raised us up on chairs, but somehow it wasn't the same. It felt almost hollow, and I don't think anyone was sorry when the DJ changed the record to the Rolling Stones.

Libby and I kept in touch for the first few years, but then life kind of gobbled each of us up. Last I'd heard, she'd had a couple of sons and was still living in Brooklyn.

I decided to give her a call. Handing Isaac back to his grandmother, I went out to the front hall, where my father had left my bags. I dug my Palm Pilot out of my purse and looked up Libby's number. Peter had given me the little electronic organizer for my last birthday. Initially, I was disappointed that the box it came in didn't contain the sapphire earrings I'd had my eyes on, but I'd quickly grown to love it. It kept all my addresses and all my appointments current and available at the touch of a button. True, I didn't actually *have* any appointments, other than the kids' doctor's visits, but if I *had* had somewhere to go, I'm sure my Palm Pilot would have helped me get there on time. I found Libby's number and went upstairs, where my voice wouldn't have to compete with the shrill giggles of my children.

Libby was home.

"Libby! You'll never guess who this is!"

"Juliet Applebaum!" she said.

I was flabbergasted. "How did you know? We haven't talked in what, seven years?"

"I think it's closer to eight. I have no idea how I knew it was you. I just recognized your voice. How are you? Where are you? Are you married? Do you have kids?"

"I'm great. I got married about five years ago. I have a daughter named Ruby, she's three, and a son named Isaac, who's just about four months. And you? I remember you had two sons. Any more kids?"

"Well, you know about Yonasan and Shaul. And then I had three more, all boys. David is five, Yiftach is three, and the baby, Binyamin, is a year and a half old. And I'm pregnant."

"Wow. Libby, that's incredible. Five boys. And another one on the way. You must be absolutely exhausted. Do you know what you're having?"

"Well, I'm a little tired, but mostly I'm just very happy. The boys all keep each other busy. I don't know what's coming this time, but I'm hoping for a girl. I think Josh would be happy if we had six more boys, but it would be lovely to have a little girl. You're so lucky. Is Ruby just a doll?"

"She's great, really, but she's hardly a doll. Unless Mattel has come out with a new extra-bossy Barbie. Ruby's a lovely kid, but she sure knows what she wants."

"My Shaul is the same way. He's under the impression that he's in charge of all the others. He even bosses his older brother around. Yonni is such a gentle soul that he does whatever Shaul tells him to."

"I imagine with five you must be home with them?"

"Of course. I haven't worked since I was pregnant with Yonni. I wouldn't want to miss any of this time. It's just so magical, don't you think?"

Magical? Well, sometimes. And a lot of the time it's boring and stressful.

"Definitely," I said aloud. "So, listen, Libby—do you live anywhere near Borough Park?"

"If right in the middle counts as near, then yes."

"Oh, wonderful. That's great. Here's the thing: I'm trying to track down a family in Borough Park. Maybe you know them, the Hirsches?"

"The head of Yeshiva B'nai B'chorim?"

"Yes, I think that must be him. I wasn't sure of the name of the yeshiva, but I know he's the head of one."

"Of course I know the Hirsches. Everyone knows the Hirsches. Or, at least, everyone knows of them."

"Do you know them or just know of them?"

"I've never met Rav Hirsch, but I actually do know his wife, Esther. Our boys are in *cheder* together."

"*Cheder*?" Libby's glottals were better than mine and I'd spent my entire childhood in Hebrew School.

"You know, like nursery school for little boys. David and her son are in the same class. I've even been to her house a few times for tea. What do you want with the Hirsches?"

"Well, it's kind of a long story. How about if I invite myself over to your house and I tell you all about it there?" Once I was ensconced in her home, maybe I could persuade Libby to introduce me to her friend."

"I'd love to see you." She sounded a little doubtful, obviously worried about what it was I was after.

I decided to just go ahead and be pushy. "Are you busy tomorrow morning? Do you think I could stop by at around, say ten-thirty or so?"

"Sure," she said, getting over whatever concerns she

might have felt. "That would be fine. I would love to see you, Juliet."

"Great! I'll see you at ten-thirty."

Before I could hang up, Libby quickly said, "Um, Juliet, remember to dress appropriately, okay? You know, modestly?"

Luckily, I'd brought along the outfit that had convinced Yossi that I was Orthodox. "No problem. I'll be so modest, you won't recognize me."

Thirteen

I had expected Borough Park, the capital of American Hasidic Judaism, to look something like the pictures I'd seen of Manhattan's Lower East Side at the turn of the century. Crowded tenements, scores of black-hatted men in sidelocks rushing to and fro. I probably wouldn't have been surprised to see the odd pushcart. Instead, as I drove my mother's car down Thirteenth Avenue, I found a bustling, commercial district like any other in the city. There were stores everywhere. Some looked like discount clothing outlets, but others were decidedly upscale. Granted, the men were wearing their black hats and coats and many did have long beards. But the women were dressed to the nines. If I didn't know that laws of modesty required them to cover their own hair with wigs, their perfectly styled coiffures would not have given them away. While there was the occasional matron in a dowdy dress, most of the women wore flattering and elegant suits with gorgeous, matching hats. They pushed huge strollers of the most expensive makes; Apricas and Peg Peregos. My neighbors back in Los Angeles looked provincial and old-fashioned by comparison.

Libby's apartment building was a huge, concrete-and-metal structure built probably in the mid-1950s. I parked in the pay lot across the street and carried Isaac into the building. I'd left Ruby in New Jersey with my parents. The lobby had a sitting area with pale pink couches, darker pink carpeting, an elaborate silk flower arrangement, and a doorman. I gave him Libby's name and apartment number and he buzzed her for us.

"A Mrs. Applebaum for you, Mrs. Bernstein," he said into the intercom. He paused for a moment and then turned to me. "Please go ahead, seventh floor."

Libby's apartment was pleasant and large. The front door opened into a living room with an oversized brown corduroy sectional couch wrapped around two walls. A large television was set into a sturdy wall cabinet, surrounded by bookshelves spilling over with titles in both Hebrew and English. The set was tuned to *Teletubbies*, and three little boys were stretched out on the floor, eyes glued to the screen. Libby turned from the door she'd opened for us and called out, "David, Yiftach, Benny, look, it's Mama's friend Juliet." The boys looked up and smiled good-naturedly but immediately turned back to their show.

"Teletubbies, feh!" Libby said. "It's one of the only shows I let them watch, so they're just crazy about it."

"Ruby loves it, too," I said.

Libby smiled and gently tapped the older boy on the behind with her foot. He giggled, and swatted her away.

I almost didn't recognize my college roommate. In fact,

if I'd bumped into her on the street I might have walked by without more than a faint feeling of having seen her somewhere before. In college, Libby had been beautiful, in kind of a horsy way. She'd had long blónd hair that fell to her shoulders and had always been swept back in a headband: denim for every day, velvet for special occasions. She was tall, probably five foot eight or so, although I'm so short that anyone over five foot two seems like a giant to me, and leggy. Now, Libby had covered her blond hair with a brown wig teased into a puff at the top of her head. She was still thin, and carried her pregnancy like a basketball stuffed under her shirt. She wore a plain navy maternity dress, and heavy support hose covered her beautiful legs. Libby looked almost exactly like your typical Hasidic matron. But she couldn't cover up the long, narrow nose that one of her ancestors had schlepped over on the *Mayflower* and proceeded to hand down to every generation of patrician New England WASPs that sprang from his loins.

"Juliet! You look exactly like you did in college!" she said.

"Yeah, exactly," I replied, "except now my hair is red, and I've gained thirty pounds. Other than that, I look exactly the same. You, on the other hand, haven't changed a bit. Well, except for the clothes. And the hair. And the pregnancy."

She patted her wig absently. "It's actually kind of ironic that I have natural blond hair that I cover with a brown wig. Half the women in the neighborhood cover up their mousy brown hair with luxurious blond wigs. I'd never do that, though. It sort of defeats the purpose of dressing modestly in the first place."

Libby led me into the kitchen. It was a bright room painted a soft yellow with children's drawings taped to the walls. There was a large white table pushed up against one wall, surrounded by eight chairs made of blond wood with woven straw seats. I sat down at the table, cradling a sleeping Isaac in my arms. Libby leaned over me and touched him gently on the cheek.

"What a sweetheart," she said.

"I hope you don't mind that I brought him. I haven't had a chance to pump any breast milk and he's never had formula."

"Not at all, not at all. What a little sleeper he is!"

"Hardly," I said. "He's only just started napping in the past week or so. And, he still wakes up all night long. Last night at my parents he woke up every hour and a half."

"That's the time change. And the unfamiliar crib. He'll adjust," Libby reassured me.

"Were your guys good sleepers?" I asked.

"Oh, we're so lucky. They all slept through the night at about six weeks."

My mouth dropped open. "I'm trying not to hate you," I said.

Libby smiled. "It has nothing to do with me, I promise you. My boys just came out like that. They're all pretty easygoing. Well, all except Shaul. He's my challenge. He's smarter than the rest of us and knows it."

We chitchatted for a while longer and then fell silent. I took a cookie from the platter that Libby had put on the table.

"So, Juliet. What's all this with the Hirsches?" she asked.

I chewed for a moment before answering. The Finkelsteins didn't want the Hirsches to know about Fraydle's disappearance because they felt that that might jeopardize her match with Ari. It was certainly not my place to give away that secret. On the other hand, what if my speculation was right? What if Fraydle's father had, despite her opposition and his wife's support of her right to make a free choice, shipped Fraydle off to the Hirsches, knowing that once the marriage took place, neither Fraydle nor her mother would do anything about it? If that was the case, and if I could find Fraydle before the wedding, then I owed it to her and to her mother to do something.

First I swore Libby to secrecy. She promised to tell no one what I was going to tell her. Then, I told her the whole story. When I finished, I looked up at her. Her face was white, except for two spots of color, high on either cheek.

"Juliet, you have some nerve," she said.

I was taken aback. "What? What are you talking about?"

"What do you think we are? Do you think we're some barbaric tribe of people? That we kidnap our children and sell them in marriage?"

"No, no—I just—"

She cut me off. "You just assumed that this man, this learned rabbi, would smuggle his child out of her mother's house and send her to be with a man she doesn't love."

That was true, I had to admit. "I know it sounds terrible, but you have to understand, Libby, the man is acting very strange. His daughter has been gone for days, but he refuses to call the police."

"Maybe because he knows her. Maybe because he knows that she ran away and he is trying to save her from herself. If the police find her and arrest her as a runaway, do you think any self-respecting man would marry her? Her father is trying to salvage a future for her out of the mess she made."

"Libby, you don't know that, any more than I know that

he sent her out here. Neither of us knows what he's capable of."

"Maybe so. Maybe I don't know him. But I do know Esther Hirsch. And I know she would never harbor a kidnapped girl, no matter how much she approved of the match. I know she'd never let her son marry a girl who didn't want to be his wife."

I didn't know what to say. Libby slapped her hand on the table. "You know what? I'm going to introduce you to this woman. I'm going to let you see for yourself whether or not she's a white slaver. But so help me Juliet, don't you dare open your mouth about your crazy ideas. You just come with me to drop David off at *cheder*. We'll tell Esther you're an old friend. You'll meet her and you'll see that she's just a loving mother and not a criminal."

"I never accused her of being a criminal," I said weakly. Libby just glared at me.

Fourteen

LIBBY lent me a stroller for Isaac, and I helped her get her boys ready to go out. We walked the few blocks to the school in silence and arrived before most of the other mothers. Libby kissed David goodbye and sent him into the classroom. After a few minutes, the other boys began arriving, and Libby introduced me to their mothers as an old friend from college. Esther Hirsch and her son Nosson came a few minutes late. She was a woman in her forties, no taller than I, and quite plump, with a prodigious shelf of a bosom. Her merry brown eyes were surrounded by laugh lines and she greeted me with a smile and a kiss on the cheek.

"Welcome. It's so lovely to meet you. Your friend Libby is very dear to me, you know!"

Libby looked surprised at the warmth of Esther's greeting but blushed happily.

Just then, Isaac woke up from his nap and began fussing.

I lifted him out of the borrowed stroller and jiggled him up and down, to no avail.

"I'm afraid I'm going to have to nurse him," I said to Libby. "Is there somewhere I could go?"

"There's the ladies' room," she said doubtfully. "But I'm not sure how clean it is."

Esther put her arm around me, and squeezed. "Don't be ridiculous. You don't want to nurse in the ladies' room. Come to my house, we live right next door. You'll nurse and we'll have a cup of tea and some cake. I made a sour cream nut cake this morning. It's still warm."

I happily agreed. Libby shot me a worried look, but she couldn't beg off without insulting her friend. The three of us gathered our assorted babies and headed off down the block.

Libby and I made ourselves comfortable at Esther's kitchen table, a lovely piece of antique pine. As I pulled out a breast for my hungry son, it occurred to me that I'd sat around more oversized kitchen tables eating kosher baked goods in the past week than I had during the course of my entire life. Esther bustled about the large kitchen, pulling china plates and cups out of the French country–style cabinets and cream out of the massive, double-door, Sub-Zero refrigerator. She cut the cake on the marble countertop and carefully laid the slices on a cut-glass serving dish. Finally, she sat down with a contented grunt, and served us each a generous slice of cake and a large cup of tea.

"So, Juliet, dear. Tell me about yourself. Where do you live? Are you observant? How many children do you have?"

I neglected to mention that my husband wasn't a member of the tribe. I started by describing Ruby's Jewish preschool. Once I'd thoroughly detailed the *succah* Ruby's class had constructed in the yard of the synagogue, I pressed Esther to tell me a little about her own kids. She happily told me all about her three sons and one daughter. They ranged in age from little Nosson up to Shira, the daughter, who, at twenty-six, was her oldest.

"Shira's married, with three of her own. My grandson Ya'akov is the same age as Nosson!" Esther said proudly.

"And your oldest son, what about him? Is he married?" I asked.

Libby ground the heel of her shoe into my foot. I plastered a smile on my face to cover my wince of agony.

"Ari's engaged," Esther said. Her tone changed just a bit. She was still smiling, but there seemed to me to be something forced about it.

"Congratulations!" I said. "When is he getting married?"

"This year," Esther said. "The girl lives in Los Angeles, like you, and she needs to prepare herself for the move. I hope that the wedding will be in four or five months. Certainly before six months."

"And is he excited about the wedding?" I asked.

"Of course," Esther said, a little too quickly. "He's thrilled. What boy wouldn't be thrilled? She's a beautiful girl from a good family. He's thrilled. Just thrilled." As if by saying so she could make it true. Had the Hirsches heard something about Fraydle that was giving Ari second thoughts about the match?

I was preparing myself to probe a little deeper when Isaac gave a contented belch and popped off my breast.

"Well, we'd better be off," Libby said hurriedly. "We don't want to keep you."

Esther smiled, but she didn't protest. There wasn't any way I could keep us there short of out-and-out rudeness, so Libby and I gathered our things, made our thank-yous, and left. As we walked down the block toward her house, Libby seemed disturbed.

"Well, there's clearly *something* going on there," I said.

"It's not what you think."

"What do you mean, it's not what I think? What is it?"

"It has nothing to do with Fraydle."

"You don't know that, Libby."

"Yes I do. Trust me, I do."

"Okay, enough of the cryptic comments. Just what the hell, er, heck, do you know?"

Libby didn't answer.

"Libby!" I stopped in my tracks. "I'm not walking another step until you tell me what's going on."

She turned back to me and sighed. "I hate doing this. It's pure *lashon hora*, evil tongue, malicious gossip. I shouldn't say anything, but I can't bear for you to think badly of that lovely woman. As if she could ever do what you think she did."

"I didn't ever say I thought she did anything knowingly."

"She didn't do anything, knowingly or not."

"Come on, Libby. What do you know?"

She paused for a minute and then, roughly scratching at her wig, said, "I'll tell you, but not here on the street. Come back to my house."

I walked as quickly as I could back to Libby's apartment with her lagging behind me. I was obviously more interested in having the conversation than she was. When we got there, she tortured me further by first settling her sons down for their nap. By the time she returned to the living room, I was going out of my mind with impatience.

She plopped down on the couch next to me and reached out for Isaac. I passed the baby to her and she held him on her knees, facing her. She kissed him a couple of times on the nose. Finally, I burst out, "Libby! Talk!"

"Okay." She handed Isaac back to me and settled herself on the couch. "Before I say anything, I want you to understand that nothing I'm telling you can go beyond this room."

"I can't promise you that, Libby. If anything happened to Fraydle, then I'm going to have to talk to the police."

"This has nothing to do with the girl!" Libby insisted. "What I'm going to tell you is about Ari."

That intrigued me. "All right, I'll tell you what. I won't tell anybody anything, unless I absolutely have to. Okay?"

That satisfied her. She nodded and began: "Josh heard a rumor about Ari from some of the other men at the *shul*, the synagogue. Last year, Rav Hirsch had a mild heart attack. It wasn't any big deal, he only stayed overnight at the hospital and then they sent him home. But the scare got people talking about who would take over the yeshiva once Rav Hirsch couldn't lead it anymore. The obvious choice is Ari. He's something of a Talmudic scholar in his own right, and he hasn't shown any interest in going into his mother's brothers' business. As soon as his name was mentioned, however, the men began talking about how he would be an "inappropriate" choice. Josh pressed them, but all they would say was that since Ari was unmarried he wouldn't be suitable. Well, at the time, the boy was only twenty-three years old. Hardly an old bachelor. Later, when they were alone, one of Josh's good friends, also a *chozer b'tshuvah,* told him what the men were talking about."

"What's a chozer b'whatever?" I interrupted.

"A *chozer b'tshuvah.* A Jew who, like Josh, comes to Orthodoxy after being raised in a secular family. It means, literally, one who returns to the answer. Since they are both *chozrei b'tshuvah*, Sam and Josh have a lot in common. Sam joined the community ten years before Josh and I did and he's been sort of a mentor to Josh. Anyway, Sam told him that there are rumors that Ari might be . . . well, that he might not like women."

"Ari's gay?" I asked.

"I don't know that," Libby said quickly. "All I'm telling you is that some of the men say that about him. It could be nothing. Maybe it's just because he's a delicate boy. You know how men are."

"Oh yeah, those rough-and-ready yeshiva *buchers*. The most macho crowd outside a tubercular ward. I can see how they'd turn on a sissy."

"That's not fair, Juliet. Just because a man is learned doesn't mean he's necessarily effeminate. Look at Josh, for example."

Now, maybe Libby was right, and maybe all male intellectuals aren't weenies, but the example of her husband, who weighed in at about ninety-eight pounds, did not lend particularly strong evidence to her claim.

"I'm not saying that they're effeminate," I explained. "I'm saying that, as a group, they aren't particularly, well, *butch*. And most of them are straight. So, it really doesn't make sense for them to have spread rumors about Ari just for being, what did you call it? Oh yeah, 'delicate.' There's got to be something more. Did Josh's friend say where the rumors started?"

"No, he didn't know. I only told you that story so you would understand why Esther might be reticent on the topic of her son's marriage. Maybe she knows people are talking about him. Maybe she has her own concerns. Whatever it is, it has nothing to do with Fraydle."

"Maybe, maybe not. What would happen if Fraydle or her family got wind of the rumors about Ari?"

"I don't know. That would depend on them. If they believed the rumors, they might call off the match. But maybe not. It depends."

"What?" I asked. "You mean they might go ahead and let her marry him?"

"Well, they would probably ask Ari to reassure them that he wasn't gay, or that if he was that it wouldn't be a problem in the marriage."

"Uh, Libby? Exactly how could that not be a problem?"

"I don't presume to know everything about homosexuality, Juliet. But I do know that if it's true that ten percent of people are homosexual, like the Queer Alliance at Wesleyan told us, then it stands to reason that there are a decent number of homosexual Hasidic Jews. But the vast majority of us marry and have children. Obviously, there are homosexual people who manage to suppress their sexual urges in favor of the rewards of family, community, and religion."

"Or else they're just deeply in the closet."

"Maybe, but what's so wrong with that? If they feel content with their family lives and happy in their community, then who's to say they're not happy? Sex isn't really that important, anyway."

"It's not just sex, Libby. Being gay isn't just a matter of who you like to sleep with. It's about who you are. How can you say that someone can be happy denying his identity solely because his community won't accept him? How do you know that those people you're talking about aren't absolutely miserable, pretending to be something they're not?" I asked.

"You're right, Juliet," Libby said. "I have no idea what they might feel. For all I know, the vast majority of gay people leave the community rather than figure out a way of being both gay and Hasidic. I don't know. I guess it's just that I'm so happy, I can't imagine that everyone wouldn't want exactly what I have: a wonderful family with beautiful children and a community in which I feel loved and protected."

"You know, Libby, that's probably all that the vast majority of gay people want, too. They want a wonderful family and a supportive community that accepts them for who they are."

"Juliet, I know that. I'm not some homophobic person. I *agree* with you. I'm just saying that for us it's more complicated."

My mind was spinning with the possibilities raised by what Libby told me. I had no idea what it all meant, or if it played any role in Fraydle's disappearance. But I definitely needed to know more.

"Libby, what you told me could be important. I'm going to need to find out more about it."

"Why? Why can't you just leave it alone?"

"Because Fraydle is missing and I have to find her."

"You? Why you? You barely even know this girl. She baby-sat for you all of one time, for goodness' sake. Why do you need to disturb this poor boy's life for someone you barely know?"

That brought me up short. Libby was right, of course. I didn't know Fraydle. The truth was that none of this was any of my business. Just like the murder of Abigail Hathaway hadn't been any of my business. But you know what? I'd never been very good at minding my own business, and I wasn't particularly interested in learning how at this late date. And it wasn't like there was someone else in New York looking for Fraydle.

"I just have to, that's all. Libby, I can do this with or without you. I can try snooping around on my own, but I can't promise to be very discreet. I don't know anyone around here, and the only way for me to get information is to ask for it. And if I'm asking strangers, that's not discreet."

"It sure isn't." Libby was scowling.

"But if you and Josh were willing to help me, then maybe I might be able to get my questions answered without causing too much of a fuss." I know, I know. Blackmail. Unpleasant, but certainly effective.

Libby sighed. "What do you want me to do?"

"I want to meet Josh's friend. The one who told him about Ari."

Libby didn't say anything.

"Libby?"

She slapped her hands on her knees. "Fine. Come to dinner tomorrow night. I'll make sure he's here."

"Libby, you're a champ." I leaned over to kiss her on the cheek. She pushed me away, at first, but finally shrugged her shoulders and rolled her eyes.

"Juliet Applebaum, you haven't changed an iota, have you?"

I shook my head and then looked down at my watch. It was getting on in the afternoon. If I wanted to miss the bridge traffic going home, I had to get started right away.

"I'd better get going," I said, picking up Isaac and standing up. Libby walked me to the door and we hugged.

I held her tight for a moment, trying to understand what was making me so sad. Suddenly, I realized that I wasn't sad for Libby. She was happy. I was sad for myself. Whatever she had, whatever it was that made her so satisfied with her life, was missing in my mine. "You know what, Libby?" I said, "I'm jealous of you. You've found a place in life where you can really be content. I don't think I know anyone who is as happy as you are."

"I know just how lucky I am, Juliet. I *am* happy. Really happy. I have a loving husband, beautiful children, and a supportive community. I have found my place. But what a funny place for a card-carrying member of the Daughters of the American Revolution!"

I laughed and said, "See you tomorrow."

"You'd better be on your best behavior, Juliet."

"I will. I promise."

She rolled her eyes again and shut the door after me.

Fifteen

THE next morning I sat at breakfast mulling over the events of the previous day and braiding Ruby's hair. Libby was right. Esther Hirsch didn't seem like the kind of person who could participate in anything nefarious. But appearances can be deceiving. It was at least possible that Fraydle's disappearance had something to do with Ari Hirsch.

"Sit still!" I said to my daughter, just barely resisting the temptation to yank on her braids. "I can't braid your hair if you keep bending over like that."

"My foot itches!" Ruby said indignantly.

My mother scooped a squirming Ruby out of my lap and held out her hand for the comb and elastics. I handed them over, relieved. I've never been much of a hairstylist. My mother sat down with Ruby, who suddenly decided to become a contender for best-behaved preschooler.

I got up to get myself another cup of coffee.

"Every drop of caffeine you drink goes directly to your breast milk," my mother said.

"Thank you, Madame La Leche, but I need coffee this morning. I'm exhausted. Your grandson was up all night, in case you hadn't noticed."

"Of course he was up. Why should he sleep? You're chock full of caffeine."

"Ma, I am so *not* going to fight with you this morning. Where's Isaac?"

"His grandfather took him for a walk. Okay, Rubileh, go look in the mirror. You look like a princess." My mother had made two braids on either side of Ruby's face. For a total of four. She looked like a lunatic.

"Just like a princess," I agreed. I leaned back and put my feet up on the kitchen table.

"Listen, Ma. I'm going to have to go back to Libby's for dinner tonight, okay? You don't mind watching Ruby again, do you?"

"Of course not, but why don't you leave Isaac, too?"

"I can't. I haven't pumped any milk for him and I really don't want him to have any baby formula."

"So pump. You brought that horrible machine. Why don't you use it?"

True, why not? I went to the pile of suitcases and pulled out my breast pump. I stripped down to my nursing bra, set the machine on the kitchen table, and attached the hoses and bottles. The first time I'd used this pump I'd had the pressure turned on full blast. It had taken a good minute and a half to extricate my nipple from the grip of the machine. A minute and a half spent screaming both in pain and in horror. Who knew my nipple could extend to a cool seven inches in length? I carefully adjusted the vacuum to the "medium" setting and settled in for a wait. Pumping has never been easy for me. I can sit for hours like some pathetic heifer and end up with a measly two ounces of milk sloshing around in the bottom of the bottle.

Today wasn't any different. I closed my eyes and imagined that the sucking and hissing of the machine was really my darling baby boy. I visualized. I meditated. And half an hour later I had three ounces of milk.

"Is that enough?" my mother asked.

"I hope so. It's all I've got."

"Here. Give it me and I'll put it in the fridge." My mother reached out to take the bottle. I waved her away.

"Don't worry, I've got it."

"No, give it to me. You're still hooked up to the milking machine."

We wrestled for the bottle and, inevitably, watched it crash to the floor between us.

"*Oy,*" she said, as the milk spilled in a tiny little pool on the floor.

"I guess the baby is coming with me tonight."

"I guess so."

"HERE'S my question for you," I said to Libby's husband's friend. "If Ari Hirsch is hiding the fact that he is gay, what would happen if that information were made public?"

We were sitting around Libby's kitchen table. Libby's children were sleeping and she was leaning against the counter, holding a dozing Isaac in her arms. She'd made roast chicken and Brussels sprouts, and we'd eaten the meal awkwardly, waiting to have this conversation. Josh's friend, Sam Kramer, had come to dinner somewhat reluctantly. I could tell he suspected my motives for asking questions about Ari Hirsch. Josh wasn't any happier to see me.

After a moment, Sam answered my question.

"I don't really know. Maybe his family would disown him. Maybe they wouldn't talk about it and hope it would just go away."

I raised my eyebrows.

"Mr. Kramer, maybe you can just give me some background here. Do you know if there are any gay Hasidic men? Are being gay and being religious mutually exclusive?"

Sam carefully wiped a crumb of strudel from the corner of his fleshy mouth. He leaned back and crossed his hands over his corpulent belly. "The way I see it, there are basically three routes open to the gay man who is also a religious Jew," he said. "First of all, he can get married and do his best to suppress his sexuality. He can fake being a heterosexual man."

"But do you think that's really possible?" I asked.

"What do I know? I imagine it's possible. If the man concentrates on the holiness of his life and not on his own needs, he might be okay."

This was more or less the scenario Libby had described. "Do you know men who live like this?" I asked.

"Not really. It's sort of a necessary corollary to that lifestyle that a man keep it all a secret, don't you think? But once I met the rabbi for the gay Jewish center in the Village. They run workshops and have meetings there. He told me they even have a group of gay yeshiva students that meets regularly."

"Really?" I was surprised.

"Really."

I thought for a moment. "It seems like Ari's parents are hoping he'll do just what you're talking about: get married and ignore it, hope it'll go away. If the rumors are true, that is."

"If he is gay, then that's probably what they want, but we don't know that he is, do we? Whatever he is or isn't, he could make the most wonderful, loving, and sensitive parent. He could be a perfect husband." Sam belched softly.

"Maybe," I said doubtfully. "You said there are three options. You described one. What are the other two?"

"He could break with the strict Hasidic community altogether. There are Modern Orthodox synagogues on the Upper West Side that would probably accept him. He might find a community there. That's more or less what that gay rabbi I told you about did. He's from a strict Orthodox family. He came out of the closet when he was in rabbinical school. You can imagine what his family thought of that. Needless to say, he's not really Orthodox anymore."

"And the last option?"

"Lastly he could remain in the community, but be on his own. He would never get married. He would live alone, or even with a man if he did it very discreetly. He would be isolated from the gay community, but he would still be a member of the religious community."

All this was very interesting, but how did it relate to Fraydle?

"Ari was getting married, so he was clearly choosing the first path. What would have happened if Fraydle's family found out?" I had asked this question of Libby, but I wanted to see if Sam's answer was any different.

"That depends. They might cancel the match. Or they

might ignore the rumors and go forward. It depends on how important the match was, and on how suited the two were for each other in other ways."

Could Fraydle and her family have heard about the rumors? Perhaps her father had pushed her to go forward despite what they'd heard. Maybe that had been her reason for running away.

"Listen, Juliet, if I were you, I'd be careful." Josh said.

"Excuse me?" I said.

"The Hirsches are an important family. And Ari's uncles on his mother's side are, well, powerful."

"I know. I heard about the rich uncles who own half of Borough Park."

"Those uncles have their own reputation. They're . . . they're not so easy to deal with."

"Josh," Sam said, a note of warning in his voice.

"What do you mean?" I pressed.

Josh looked at Sam and shrugged his shoulders. "Nothing really. It's just that they're real estate guys. They collect their own rents."

"What? Like they're Jewish mobsters or something?"

"No! No! Nothing like that. All I'm saying is that you shouldn't mess around with these guys. They might not like someone asking questions about their nephew."

I looked at Josh for a moment, wondering if he was serious. Was he really telling me to watch out for a couple of old Hasidic men? I thanked him for his warning and assured him I would be careful. I almost told him that after being shot once, I wasn't likely to put myself in that position again, but I decided that I didn't have the time for the explanations that comment would require.

What he said did make me think of something else, however. Maybe Fraydle had found out about Ari and threatened not only to call off the match, but also to tell people why she was doing it. How far would the uncles have gone to ensure her silence?

"I need to talk to Ari Hirsch. Can you arrange that for me?"

Libby, who had been silent throughout our conversation, interrupted. "No. That's ridiculous. Why do you need to talk to this boy? Why do you need to bother him? You'll just scare him with this."

"Look, Libby, all I know right now is rumor and innuendo. I need to know the truth, and I need to find out what Fraydle knew. The only way that I can think of to do this is to talk to Ari."

"Ridiculous," Sam blustered.

"Not ridiculous at all," I said. "The other option is to ask Fraydle's family. Which do you think would bother Ari more?"

The three looked at each other for a moment. Finally, Josh spoke. "I can't promise he'll talk to you. But I can tell him who you are. The rest is up to you."

sixteen

JOSH agreed to speak to Ari the next day. Libby handed Isaac to me and stiffened when I hugged her. She did not return my embrace. I hoped I hadn't lost a friend.

I found Ruby still awake and waiting for us at my parents' front door.

"Hi, kiddo," I said. "Did you have fun with Grandma and Grandpa? Did you go visit Bubba in the nursing home?"

She nodded, but, with a trembling lip, whispered, "I miss Daddy."

I handed Isaac to my mother and scooped Ruby up in my arms. I kissed her on the cheek. She buried her face in my neck and started to cry.

I said, "I know, honey. It's hard to be away from Daddy. I miss him, too. Should we give him a call?" We'd already spoken to Peter about three hundred times in the two days we'd been gone, but another call wouldn't hurt. I settled her on one hip and reached for the phone. I dialed Peter's cell phone number, since I was pretty sure I'd find him on the set.

It rang twice and then a female voice answered, "Hi!"

I felt a wave of intense jealousy crash over me, utterly obliterating all the good feelings generated by our loving moments at Miserable Mindy's party and at the airport. Now, I know that my husband is crazy about me, and I know that he would never cheat on me. But there's something about being postpartum, even four months postpartum, that makes you feel vulnerable. The problem isn't that you're still carrying around that extra pregnancy weight, although that doesn't help. It's not even that sleep deprivation has etched permanent black smudges under your eyes and in your mood. The real problem is that the very last thing in the universe you feel like doing is touching any human being other than your baby, and that includes your husband. When you're a nursing mother, your body belongs to someone else. You are perpetually available to satisfy the physical demands of your baby. The idea of satisfying another person's physical desires, no matter how much fun that might end up being for you personally, is just too much. At least that's how I felt. There I was, a woman who loved her husband desperately but who had about as much interest in sex as in skydiving; less, in fact. And there she was, whoever she was, with her breathy little "Hi!"

"This is Juliet. Is my *husband* there?" Icicles dangled from my words.

"Juliet! It's so wonderful to hear from you! We were just wondering how you and your adorable kids are doing!"

We? "Who is this?" I asked, not defrosting in the least.

"Oh, I'm sorry. This is Mindy Maxx."

"No, *I'm* sorry," I replied. "I thought I dialed Peter's cell phone. I must have gotten your number by mistake."

Mindy and I both knew that I didn't know her cell phone number. Obviously, I couldn't really believe I'd miraculously dialed it instead of Peter's. She would have had to be a total moron not to understand how angry and suspicious I was.

She wasn't an idiot. "Juliet, I just picked up Peter's phone. We're in the production trailer going over the rushes and I just picked it up off the table where he left it. Honestly."

There was a scuffling noise and then Peter's voice came on the line.

"Hey, honey!" he said. "Sorry about that. Mindy just grabbed my phone as a joke."

"Ha ha ha," I said.

He paused, as if he was trying to figure out why I was upset. Are all men this clueless? "Let's talk about this later, okay?" he said.

"Whatever. Your daughter wants to talk to you." I handed Ruby the phone and walked out of the kitchen, tears in my eyes. I grabbed Isaac from my mother and sat down on the couch and buried my nose in his soft little neck. He giggled deliciously.

"*You* love me best, don't you?" I whispered in his ear.

He grabbed a clump of my hair and shoved it in his mouth. I listened while Ruby chatted animatedly with her father. That little girl sure loved her Daddy.

"What's wrong, *mamaleh*?" my father asked, leaning forward in his chair. He patted me on the knee. "Did Peter say something?"

"No," I sighed. "I'm just jealous of Mindy, his new best friend."

"What are you jealous for? You're a beautiful woman. You're the mother of his children. What do you care if he has some friend? He loves *you*!"

"I know. It's just that things haven't been very much fun around the house lately. I can't blame him for enjoying her company more than mine. At least she doesn't smell like spit-up. And I'm not beautiful, by the way." Now I was fishing.

"Yes, you are. You're gorgeous. Lovely. A little *zaftig*, maybe, but that's very attractive. Who wants to sleep with a bag of bones?"

Great. Even my own father thought I was fat.

"For God's sake, Gene," my mother said, whacking my father on the back of the head with a magazine. "She's not *zaftig*! What are you saying? *Zaftig*. You idiot."

"Stop hitting me!"

"What hitting? I tapped you on the head. I should show you hitting."

By now I'd stopped crying and was just laughing. My parents, the Jewish Honeymooners. I handed Isaac to my dad and went back into the kitchen. I took the phone away from Ruby, unwinding her from the cord she'd managed to wrap around her neck and waist.

"Hi. Sorry," I said.

"Me, too," Peter said. "Why don't you come home so we can fight in person? That way we'd at least get to have make-up sex."

"We could have make-up phone sex." I suggested.

"Hmm. Maybe. Where are your parents?"

"Right here."

"Never mind."

"We're coming home soon."

"I know. I love you, Juliet."

I started to cry again. "I know. I love you, too."

"I love you too, too."

"I love you too, too, too."

"Oh, for God's sake," my mother said, pushing past me into the kitchen. "What are you, a couple of teenagers? You miss him so much, you should go home."

"I don't want to go home. I want to stay here and watch you and Daddy hit each other with newspapers."

"It wasn't a newspaper! I tapped him with a magazine. You and your father. The two of you should go down to City Hall and get yourselves a restraining order."

I laughed. "Hey, Peter? Have I ever told you how insane my parents are?"

"I figured that out all by myself," he said. "Listen, I'd better go. We're in the middle of something."

"Okay, honey. I'll talk to you tomorrow."

We hung up.

My mother was pulling covered dishes out of the refrigerator. "I'm heating up leftover chicken for a little late-night snack," she said.

"Sounds fine to me."

"You should go visit Bubba tomorrow morning."

"I will."

"So how did it go today? Did you find your girl, what's her name? Fruma?"

"Fraydle. No, I didn't. I don't think she's in New York." I recounted my conversation with Sam.

"Sounds to me like you need to speak to that boy," my mother said.

"I thought of that myself. I asked Josh, Libby's husband, to call him for me."

"Why not just call him yourself?"

"That's a terrible idea, Mom. What am I going to say,

'Hi there, Ari. Are you queer and did you make your fiancée disappear by any chance?' "

"Don't be ridiculous. Why don't you just ask him if he'll meet you for a cup of coffee? Then you can delicately ask him about Fraydle."

"Right. Like this yeshiva *bucher* is going to meet some strange woman for coffee."

"Fine. Don't take my advice. What do I know? I'm just an old woman. You're the detective."

"I am *not* a detective."

"No. You just solve murders in your spare time."

"Exactly. I mean, no! I don't solve murders. I did solve that one before Isaac was born, but this isn't a murder. I don't even know if Fraydle is dead!"

"Who's dead? Daddy?" Ruby asked, soundly bizarrely unperturbed at the thought.

"Nobody's dead! Daddy's fine! He's just in California!"

"Don't yell at me! Yell at Grandma, not me!"

I knelt down and gave her a hug. "Sorry, honey." I kissed the top of her head. Then I walked over to my mother, put my arm around her, and kissed her on the cheek. "Sorry, Ma."

"What sorry? You don't need to be sorry. Don't be silly."

Seventeen

THE next morning I woke up late and found my mother sitting in the living room, holding the telephone receiver up to a gurgling Isaac's mouth.

"What are you doing?" I asked.

"Isaac is talking to his daddy," she said.

"Sounds like a scintillating conversation. Here, give me the phone."

I took the receiver out of her hand and made myself comfortable on the couch. Isaac immediately started nuzzling me, and I settled him across my lap.

"Hi, honey," I said, into the phone.

"Hi, baby. I'm glad I caught you."

"Isaac not enough of a conversationalist for you?"

"Not at all. He's great. He burped twice and I swear he said 'Dada.' "

"He did not. He's only four months old."

"Well, all I know is what I heard. What are you wearing?"

"What?"

"What are you wearing right now?"

I laughed. "Um, my father's green flannel nightshirt."

"Underneath?"

"Peter!"

"C'mon! Tell me."

"I can't. My mother's sitting right here."

My mother shook her head, sighed dramatically, and hoisted herself off the couch. "I'm going upstairs," she said, and stomped away.

"Okay, she's gone. Nothing."

"Mmm. Come home."

"Where are you? It's six in the morning California time. Are you at home?" I asked.

"No, I'm in the production office. I've been here all night."

"Is Mindy there?"

"Oh, for God's sake, Juliet! You really are insane. Of course she's not here. Would I be talking to you about your naked body if Mindy were here?"

I didn't say anything.

"Juliet. When are you going to figure out that I love *you*? You're the one I'm dreaming about. It's *your* body that I'm thinking about."

I sighed. "I know. I'm sorry. Again. As usual. I'm always sorry." And I was, really, it just seemed like Peter and Mindy were spending so much time together. "Listen," I said, "let's not talk about Mindy, or my body for that matter. Let me tell you about yesterday."

After I told Peter about everything I'd discovered I

asked him what he thought my next move ought to be.

"Well, if I were writing this as a screenplay," he said, "I'd want to know what your motivation was. What do you want to know? What information are you missing?"

I thought for a minute. "I guess what I need to know now is if Fraydle knew about Ari, and if she did, what, if anything, she did about it. Was she planning on going forward with the marriage? What did her parents know? Were they planning on going forward?"

"Well, you can't ask her, because she's still missing. She *is* still missing, isn't she?"

"I assume so. Nettie has my number here. She promised to call if Fraydle came home or if anything else happened." I didn't say what the anything else was, but Peter and I both knew what I meant: if she turned up dead.

"Okay, so you can safely assume she's still missing. So you can't ask her. Her father isn't likely to tell you."

"And I know Nettie would have told me if she knew anything about it. At least, I think she would have."

"So who does that leave? The mother?"

"She won't talk."

"Then who?"

"Ari Hirsch."

"So call Ari Hirsch."

"God! You and my mother. That's just what she suggested that I do. I'll tell you what I told her: I asked Josh to call him for me."

"Don't wait for Josh. Do it yourself."

And I did.

I found Ari's parents' telephone number by using my keen detective skills and calling directory assistance. Once I reached Esther, I claimed to be a clerk at a store where Ari had placed an order and asked to speak to him.

"What kind of order?" Ari's mother said.

"It's a gift order, Mrs. Hirsch," I replied. "Mr. Hirsch specifically asked us not to tell what it was. Are you his wife?"

"No, his mother."

"Well, then I certainly can't tell you, can I?" As soon as the words left my mouth I felt horribly guilty, imagining Esther waiting day after day for the surprise gift from her son, which would never arrive.

"He's at the yeshiva all day today."

A boy's high-pitched voice answered the phone at the yeshiva.

"Can I speak to Ari Hirsch, please?" I asked.

"I'll transfer you to the rabbi's office. He's in there, studying."

A moment later a soft voice answered the phone.

I swallowed, a little nervously. I've had conversations with bank robbers, drug dealers, and even the worst scum of the earth, confidential informants, but for some reason this particular conversation, with a young man I imagined to be skinny and acne-covered, hunched over his sacred texts and doubting his sexuality, made me tense.

"Is this Ari Hirsch?"

"Yes, who is this?"

"Mr. Hirsch, Ari, my name is Juliet Applebaum. I'm a friend of Fraydle Finkelstein."

"Yes. I know about you. Josh Bernstein spoke to me this morning in *shul*."

So Josh had come through.

"Ari, is there any way we can meet? I have some questions to ask you and I'd rather do it in person."

"Meet?"

"This is very urgent. Very. Please trust me. I must talk to you about Fraydle. It's an emergency."

He didn't respond.

"I'm taking my kids to the Museum of Natural History, today," I said. "Would you meet me there? We can talk for just a moment or two?"

The mention of my kids seemed to reassure him. He said, tentatively, "It is urgent, correct?"

"Very."

"I must study this morning. I can meet you this afternoon at three o'clock."

"Terrific," I said. "In the elephant room. Right under the tusks of the lead elephant. I'll be there with my two small children, a baby and a little girl."

"Under the elephant," he said, and hung up the phone.

When I hung up I looked up at my mother. She was standing over me, smiling complacently.

"What?" I said.

"A ridiculous idea," she said.

"What was?"

"Calling him. Ridiculous, you told me."

"Okay. Not ridiculous. A good idea. A very good idea. So, do you want to come into the city with me?"

"No. I have to go to the office for a few hours. Myron has a petition for certiorari due this afternoon and I can't trust the temp to get it right. You only have one chance you know. If it's late, it's late. The Supreme Court doesn't take excuses."

"I know, Ma. I filed a few of those while I was the federal public defender."

"Of course you did," she said, clearly mourning my lost days as a professional.

"Maybe Daddy will want to come along."

"Sure he will. He loves the museum."

WHEN we got to the Upper West Side we parked the car and unloaded the kids. My father insisted on putting Isaac on his own chest in the Baby Bjorn. I was sorry I hadn't brought my camera along to catch the two of them waddling down the street with Ruby skipping along next to them, her little hand buried in her Grandpa's furry paw.

It was one of those perfect New York City autumn days. The air was cool and crisp and the sun shone brightly. The city looked new and polished and smelled like apples and the streets were so clean, the asphalt seemed to sparkle. Even the homeless people looked a little more cheerful than usual. I gave Ruby a couple of dollars to distribute among them on our way down the block. My usual rule is that I give money only to women, and then only if they don't seem visibly intoxicated, but today I let Ruby hand out the bills to whomever she pleased. I wasn't sure I should be letting her play Lady Bountiful this way, but I figured it wouldn't hurt for her to understand that since she was lucky enough to have money, she had an obligation to share some of it with those who weren't as fortunate.

We walked into the beautiful old Museum of Natural History and made our way to the huge hall where the herd of elephants stands, massive and imposing, in the center of the room. I sat down on a bench under the looming tusks of the lead elephant. Ruby came up and, leaning against me, stared up into the behemoth's face.

"These elephants are all dead, right?" she asked.

"Yup," I said.

"Somebody killed them," she stated.

"That's true."

"Even the baby?"

"Even the baby."

"Why?"

"Well, Rubes, a long time ago, people didn't know that it was bad to kill animals. When these elephants were shot, people didn't really understand that if you kill lots of animals, there won't be any left."

"They'll be stink."

"What?"

"Stink. Like the dinosaurs."

"Right, exactly, *extinct*. People didn't understand about extinction and endangered species back when these elephants were killed."

"But now we know that's bad, right?"

"Right."

"And nobody kills elephants anymore. Cuz it's bad."

I wasn't about to get into a discussion of wild animal poaching and the insatiable Asian market for things like elephant tusk and rhino horn, particularly since one of my last clients was a Chinese bear-bile smuggler. So I just said, "Right."

Ruby scampered off to play with her grandpa, and I looked up. Across the room I saw a young man dressed in the garb of a Hasidic Jew. He wore a Fedora, a dark suit, and his *tzitzit* hung outside his trousers. His long sidelocks were tucked behind his ears and a patchy, light brown beard covered his chin. His cheeks were reddened with acne and pitted with scars. For all that, he wasn't unattractive. He had big blue eyes with long lashes and a straight nose. His full lips looked almost bruised under the mantle of his moustache.

I lifted my hand in a sort of half wave and he walked over to me.

"Ari Hirsch?" I asked.

"Yes. And you are Mrs. . . . uh, Mrs. . . ."

"Applebaum."

"Yes, of course. Mrs. Applebaum. A friend of Fraydle's." He stood awkwardly, a few feet from me.

"Would you like to sit down?" I motioned to the bench on which I sat. He perched at the far end, carefully maintaining a respectable distance from me.

"Did Josh Bernstein tell you why I asked you to meet me?"

"Why don't you tell me yourself," he said, his voice soft.

How was I going to do this? One of the reasons I was here was my suspicion that Ari and his family might know something about Fraydle's whereabouts. But what if he didn't? Fraydle's family was adamant about keeping her disappearance a secret from the Hirsches. How could I ask him if he knew where she was without giving away their secret? How could I ask him whether she knew about his sexual orientation without making him aware that *his* secret was out? I could do neither.

I've always believed that it's secrecy that causes the most difficulties. If you are honest and open about your problems, then nobody can hurt you by disclosing them. I didn't believe that either the Finkelsteins or Ari were doing themselves any favors by being so reticent. Now, maybe that decision wasn't mine to make, but I decided to act as if it were. For the purposes of this conversation, at least.

"Ari, I don't know how much Josh told you, but Fraydle

has disappeared. Her parents don't want your family to know; they're afraid your parents will call off the match. But she's been gone for almost a week now, and I am very worried."

"Gone? What do you mean, gone?"

"Gone as in she's not at home and nobody knows where she is."

"Could she have been kidnapped? What do the police say?"

"For the time being, Rabbi Finkelstein is conducting the search on his own."

"No police?"

"No."

"So she has just run away? Nobody has . . . has hurt her?"

"Nobody knows where she is, Ari. That's why I asked you here to talk to me. I wonder if you might know if she has run away and if so, why."

He shook his head vigorously. "I know nothing. I have met her only a few times. I don't really know her at all."

I took a breath. "Ari, there's no easy way for me to ask this. Did you tell Fraydle that you might be a homosexual?"

The blood drained from his face. He looked at me for a moment, stricken.

"Ari? Did you tell her?"

He reached his hand to a sidecurl and tugged at it nervously.

"Ari?"

"How do you know? What did she tell you about me?" he whispered.

I said nothing. I felt guilty about letting him think that Fraydle was the source of my suspicions, but I'd promised Libby and Josh that I would keep their confidence.

Ari shook his head, as if to clear his ears of my words.

"I'm not . . . not . . . I'm not what you said," he murmured.

"Ari, I'm not judging you, and I'm not going to tell anybody what I found out. All I need to know is whether you told Fraydle anything."

He remained silent for another moment, winding his hair around his finger. Finally, he turned to me and said, "Fraydle knew everything there is to know. I told her about my doubts about . . . about myself. We talked about it and we decided that with her help, and God's, I could overcome this."

That was a surprise. I guess I'd been expecting to hear that he'd told Fraydle, and her shock and her fear of marrying a man who would rather be with another man had made her run away from home. I hadn't expected to hear that the two of them had discussed the issue openly and nonetheless reached an agreement to marry.

"She agreed to go forward with the wedding?"

"Not at first. She was upset at first. But she didn't reject me right away. She told me she needed some time to think."

"Then what happened?"

"I went back to New York. She called me on the telephone, a few days later. She told me that she had thought about it and that we should marry."

"Ari, did she tell her parents?"

He shook his head. "No. We agreed to keep the secret between us."

"Are you sure she kept this agreement?"

"Yes. She promised not to tell her parents. I don't think she would have broken her promise."

"Did she tell you anything about herself, of her own doubts about marriage?"

Ari didn't take his eyes off the long thin fingers knotted in his lap. He shook his head.

It surprised me that despite the fact that her fiancé had been so honest with her, Fraydle had failed to confide in him about Yossi. However, the truth was that none of this helped me at all. If Fraydle and Ari had worked this out between them, there was no reason for her to run away. A chill ran across the back of my neck. Since the first days of Fraydle's disappearance, I'd done my best to think of her as a runaway. But I'd always known that the odds were good, and getting better with each day, that she hadn't run anywhere. It was all too possible that someone had taken her, had done something to her. Maybe that someone was sitting next to me under the elephant tusks. Or maybe that someone was in Borough Park or back in Los Angeles. I had to get on a plane to Los Angeles as soon as possible. I needed to see the Finkelsteins and convince them to go to the police. And if the rabbi refused, I would make the report myself.

The young man interrupted my thoughts. "What are you going to do?" he asked.

"Don't worry, Ari. I'm not going to tell anyone about you. I'm just trying to find Fraydle."

"You must call me as soon as you know anything."

"I will. Of course I will. Thank you for talking to me."

"No, thank *you*. Thank you for telling me. You said you are a friend of Fraydle's?" He looked at me, obviously not understanding what I, a non-Hasidic woman in a pair of overalls, could have to do with his wife-to-be.

"She was my baby-sitter." It was, I knew, a ridiculously thin connection. Not a friend. Not a member of my family. Just a girl who watched my baby one morning. So that I could take a nap.

"Ah, yes. Well, goodbye," he said.

"Goodbye, Ari."

I rushed off to where my father was standing with the kids, looking at a diorama of the African veldt.

"Look, Mama," Ruby said, "A Thompson's gazelle."

I looked at the sign next to the exhibit box. Lo and behold, it was, in fact, a Thompson's gazelle.

"How do you know what a Thompson's gazelle looks like?" I asked.

"The Kratt Brothers told me!" she replied. Thank goodness for public television.

I hustled the three of them through the rest of the museum as fast as I could, zipping by the dinosaurs and the giant blue whale. I wanted to get back to New Jersey and call the airline. The fates were conspiring against me, however, and we ended up stuck on the West Side Highway, creeping slowly north toward the George Washington Bridge. It took almost ninety minutes to get home. Luckily, Isaac fell asleep in the back of the car, after he'd screamed for an hour at the top of his lungs.

When he finally crashed into slumber, my father looked at me and said, "For a minute there I thought he'd shatter the windshield."

Eighteen

By the time we pulled into my parents' driveway, it was dark. As my father and I unloaded the kids from the car, I noticed a big black Cadillac pulled up in front of the house. The car stuck out like a sore thumb in a neighborhood where my parents' Chrysler was the only American car that wasn't a sports utility vehicle.

I lumbered up the porch stairs with a sleeping Isaac draped over my shoulder and Ruby wrapped around my leg. A group of Hasidic men stood waiting outside the front door. All wore hats, but only a few were bearded. They did not look particularly friendly.

"Hello? Can I help you?" I asked. My father, who had been coming up the steps behind me, said, at the same time, "Who are all these people?"

A large man with a big belly stepped forward. He

pointed a finger at me. "You are Juliet Applebaum," he said, rather than asked.

"Well, you're ahead of me, sir. You know who I am, but I don't know who you are," I said, trying not to show how nervous I was. I did a quick head count. There were six men standing on the porch. I decided to pretend this was a social call.

"Why don't we go inside so I can get the baby out of the cold." I walked by the man who'd spoken to me and unlocked the front door. My father followed me, reaching out for Ruby's hand.

"What's going on?" he whispered as he walked past me into the house.

"I have no idea," I answered, in a loud, clear voice.

I held the door open and the men filed in, one by one. I walked into the living room area and sat down on the couch, still holding the baby on my lap.

"Daddy," I said, "why don't you go set Ruby up with a video, upstairs."

He nodded and led her away. Meanwhile, the men had followed me across the floor and stood in a little huddle in the center of the living room. I looked them over. There were two older men, the big one who'd spoken to me and another of about the same size, but with a long, grizzled beard. The four other men were much younger. Two looked to be about my age, and two seemed no more than boys. One of the younger men, with short blond hair, a trimmed beard, and broad shoulders, looked vaguely familiar. Where had I seen him before?

"Please sit down," I said.

They all looked at the leader of the pack, who shook his head angrily. "We are not staying in this house. We came only to warn you, Juliet Applebaum. Stay away from the Hirsch family. You are not welcome."

Ah. The uncles.

"You must be Esther Hirsch's brother. It's a pleasure to meet you," I said. Here's the thing about having been a public defender: After a while, scary guys just don't scare you anymore. My clients had almost all been scary guys. They were gangbangers with elaborate tattoos, jittery bank robbers with thousand-dollar-a-day smack habits, car-jackers with arsenals of Glock 9mm semi-automatics. As their lawyer, and often the only person who really cared about what happened to them, I almost always became their confidante, confessor, and even their friend. I'd learned to look behind the crime and see the man. And the person standing in front of me, for all that he looked intimidating and even dangerous, was just a man. An old Jewish man. Like my father, but with a fur hat.

"Who I am is not important!" my rude visitor bellowed. My father came running downstairs at the sound of the shout.

"Daddy, please go up and stay with Ruby," I said.

"But—" he began.

"Daddy! I need you to stay with her. I don't want her to be scared." Though clearly reluctant, he headed back up the stairs.

I turned to the spokesman, who was pointing a finger in my face. "Stop shouting," I said. "You'll wake the baby."

The blond man, the one who looked familiar, stepped forward. "We are here to ask you to refrain from prying into the affairs of Ari Hirsch. That is all." He spoke with a faint accent.

"Ask nothing!" the leader shouted. "We are telling you! Mind your own business, you *churva*!"

At that moment, the front door opened and my mother walked in the door.

"*Churva*?" she said. "Did I hear someone say the word *churva* in my house? What's going on here?" She looked at me, and at the group of men still standing in the middle of the living room. "Josef?" she said. "Josef Petrovsky, what are you doing here? What is your mother going to say when I tell her your friend called my daughter a whore?"

Nineteen

MY mother's scolding seemed momentarily to take the wind out of the sails of my second-cousin-twice-removed and his cabal of hostile Hasidim. Then the leader raised his fist. "This is a warning," he bellowed.

The older man with the grizzled beard, who had been silent up until then, put a restraining hand on his cohort's arm. He turned to me and, in a voice made somehow more ominous by its softness, said, "We are a close family." I didn't answer. "We protect each other."

"That's nice," I said. "But what does that have to do with me?"

He smiled thinly. "You should know this about us, that is all."

"Listen, you," my mother squawked. "What do you think you are, the Jewish Gambini family? I want you out of my house. All of you. Out now, or I'm calling the police."

The quiet man ignored her and looked at me. I stood my ground.

"I think you should leave," I said.

"Out, out!" My mother grabbed the young man closest to her by the arm and began pushing him in the direction of the door. He shook her off with a rough jerk and she stared at him, her mouth open.

"Please leave," I repeated.

"Yes," the soft-voiced man said. "And you, of course, will no longer make my nephew a subject of your conversation." I said nothing. "Good. That is settled. Thank you for your time." He nodded once and walked to the front door. He waited for a moment for one of the young men to open it for him, and then walked out the door, followed by the others. My cousin was the last to leave. He walked over to my mother but she pushed him away. "Out of my house, Josef Petrovsky. You are no longer welcome here!" He slunk out the door.

"Humph!" my mother said.

"Yeah, no kidding. Hey, Ma?"

"Yes, darling?"

"What the hell was that about?"

"You're asking me? You're the one out raking muck. You tell me what happened."

"First of all," I said, "muckraking is investigative journalism. I'm not raking muck. Second of all, what was cousin Josef Petrovsky doing in our house? And why was he with Ari Hirsch's uncles?"

She shrugged her coat off her shoulders and tossed it over a chair. "First of all, that sure looked like muck to me. Second of all, I haven't any idea what Josef was doing with those horrible men."

"But you know why he was here?"

"I talked to Bella Petrovsky, Josef's mother, this morning. You've met her, darling. At Tante Tsunya's funeral years ago, when you still lived in New York. For that matter, that's where you met Josef for the first time."

I gritted my teeth in exasperation. "Ma! What did you tell her?"

"I told her you needed Josef's help."

"That's all?"

She busied herself with picking lint off her skirt.

"Ma!"

"So maybe I told her that you thought that this boy, Ari Hirsch, was a homosexual and did she ever hear any rumors about him from her son, about whom, incidentally, I've always had my doubts."

"Oh, for God's sake, Mom."

"Look, darling, how was I supposed to know that Josef knew Ari Hirsch's uncles? What, all observant Jews know each other now? Josef manages apartment buildings, for God's sake. What does he know from rabbis?"

"Oh, Mom. Ari's *father* is a rabbi. His uncles are in real estate. Josef probably works for them."

My mother put her hand to her throat. "You think?"

"Yeah, I think. Here, take the baby." I handed Isaac to her. "I'd better go upstairs and make sure Daddy and Ruby haven't barricaded themselves into a closet."

I found Ruby happily watching *101 Dalmatians* perched on my father's lap, his arms crossed protectively over her chest. He jumped about three feet into the air when I walked into the room. "All clear, Pop," I said.

"Oh, thank God. What a nightmare. Were they armed?" he asked.

"Oh, Daddy, don't be ridiculous. They were not packing heat."

"*I'm* ridiculous?" He put his hands over Ruby's ears. "I'm not the one who's been shot, young lady." Ruby squawked and batted at his hands.

"I can't hear!" she shrieked.

"Sorry, *maydele*," he said, taking away his hands and kissing the top of her head. She settled back against his chest.

"It's okay, Grandpa. I still love you," Ruby said.

I left the pair to Cruella DeVil and went to the telephone. I wanted to warn Ari Hirsch that his uncles knew that I had been looking for him. When I told him, he seemed resigned rather than upset, and I hung up the phone wondering if my search for Fraydle had accomplished anything other than making a confused young man's life that much more difficult. I then called the airline and managed to book us on a flight for the next morning. We were going to have to make two transfers and the trip would take us thirteen hours door to door, but we'd be home by tomorrow night. My parents weren't surprised at my decision, although they did extract a promise from me that we'd be back again in a couple of months. When I called Peter, he sounded overjoyed and promised to pick us up at the airport.

About the trip home I won't say anything other than that babies cry most when planes take off and land because of the change in cabin pressure. And we took off and landed six separate times. If I'd had any doubts about Isaac's lung capacity before the trip, they were entirely dispelled.

Twenty

THE morning after we got home was a Sunday. Upon waking, Ruby begged to be taken to the Santa Monica Pier and Peter happily agreed to drive her. Isaac and I unpacked and then headed out to Nettie's store. I needed to find out what was happening with the search for Fraydle and if Fraydle had told Nettie anything about Ari.

Nettie was behind the counter, as usual. She shouted my name when she saw me and rushed out to hug me.

"Did you find anything?" she whispered in my ear, eyeing her waiting customers.

"Maybe. I don't know," I replied.

"Wait!" she said, and hurried back around the counter. She quickly checked out her customers, virtually chasing out one or two who were lingering in the aisles. Then she locked the door and turned the CLOSED sign around.

"Come! To the back!" Nettie motioned me toward the

storeroom. I wheeled Isaac's stroller through the narrow doorway and she shut the door behind us.

"Now. Tell me."

"First of all, you tell *me*. I take it Fraydle hasn't come home."

Nettie shook her head, her wig jiggling back and forth with the motion.

"Has Rabbi Finkelstein called the police?"

"Not yet. If she's not home by *Shabbos*, he will. That's what Sima says. She says they must call by Friday afternoon."

"Nettie, today is only Sunday. Friday is a long way off."

"I know, I know. I'll talk to him again today. I'll try to convince him to call."

"Good."

"Juliet, did you see the Hirsches? Have they heard from Fraydle?"

"I met Esther Hirsch, and I'm pretty confident that she doesn't know anything about Fraydle's disappearance. I also met her brothers and, frankly, they are a couple of nasty guys. And I met Ari. That's what I want to talk to you about, Nettie. Did Fraydle ever tell you anything about Ari?"

"What do you mean?"

"Did she ever tell you she didn't want to go through with the marriage?"

"At the beginning, yes. She didn't even want to meet Ari Hirsch. I was worried she would reject him like she did the others."

"And she didn't?"

Nettie paused. "No, not really. I remember she asked her father if she had to marry. She asked him about the match and he told her how important it was for the family. And then she agreed to meet the boy. After they'd met a few times, she agreed to marry him."

I didn't want to give away Ari's secret to Fraydle's family. On the other hand, it seemed that Nettie was Fraydle's closest confidante.

"Nettie, did Fraydle ever confide in you any concerns she had about Ari? About his . . . um . . . his suitability as a husband?"

She paused and looked at me. "What do you mean?" she asked.

"I heard some rumors about Ari. Rumors that he might be gay."

"Gay?" she asked, confused.

"Homosexual."

"*Oy yoy yoy!*" Nettie exclaimed. "That is what she was talking about!"

"What? Did she say something to you?"

"She asked me what it meant for a man to lie with another man like it says in the *Tanach*. She asked me if it was true that some men had feelings for other men. She asked me if I knew men like this."

I leaned forward eagerly. "And what did you tell her?" I asked.

"I told her that sometimes men are like this, but that it is an abomination in the eyes of God."

She said the last so matter-of-factly.

"What did Fraydle say to that?" I asked.

"She asked me if those feelings were permanent, or if a man like that could become normal if he chose to."

"And what did you tell her?"

"Well, I thought maybe she saw something, or maybe she heard someone talking, maybe one of the young boys. So I told her that I had heard that sometimes the yeshiva *buchers* did things like that, but that it was very wicked. I told her that grown men, married men, never did that. I told her that as soon as they married, all that stopped."

I looked into Nettie's face. She looked almost defiant. "Nettie, do you really believe that?"

She shrugged her shoulders. "Why should a young, innocent girl hear about such things? Why shouldn't I reassure her?"

"Well, Nettie, do you really think she would be happy in a marriage to a homosexual man?"

"Why not? If he was a good father, and a good husband? If he could give her children? What difference does it make what he feels in his heart, as long as he follows the law?"

Never before had I felt the gulf between Nettie and me so deeply. Our beliefs were completely at odds. There was no point in arguing over this issue.

"Did you tell Fraydle's parents about your conversation?"

"No! Of course not. The girl confided in me. I wouldn't tell. Anyway, I had no idea she was talking about Ari. I'm telling you, I thought she maybe saw something or heard something," Nettie said.

I left the store, puzzling over what I'd learned. I had confirmed what Ari had told me. He'd been honest with Fraydle and she'd been reassured by her aunt. Fraydle had agreed to the match and made peace with it. So why had she disappeared? What had happened to her?

Twenty-one

RUBY and Peter were waiting for us when Isaac and I got home. I fed the baby and, when he fell asleep, carefully transferred him from my arms to his bassinet, holding my breath, hoping against hope that he wouldn't rouse. For a moment it looked like he was about to wake up, but with a grunt and a wiggle, he settled himself back to sleep.

Peter and Ruby were in the living room, playing a game called Newborn Babies. It consisted entirely of the pair of them wailing like infants.

"Mama! Let's pretend you're the mommy and I'm the baby!" Ruby shouted when I walked in the room.

"You know what, kiddo? I *am* the mommy. It's not really very much fun to pretend to be what you already are."

My daughter looked at me, puzzled, and, with a shrug of her shoulders, turned back to her father.

"Daddy, you be the daddy, and I'll be the newborn baby."

"Okay," Peter said. "Newborn baby, it's time to sleep." She collapsed on the ground and he tucked one of Isaac's blankets around her. "Night-night, newborn baby," he said.

"Waaaa," she wailed softly, and then began to pretend-snore.

Peter and I settled back on the couch and I nestled my head against his shoulder.

"What did the aunt have to say?" he asked.

I told him about Fraydle's conversation with Nettie. "I'd like to know if Yossi knew about this," I said.

"What difference would that make?" Peter asked. "Even if he knew, that doesn't put you any closer to finding out if he or anyone else did her harm."

"It's possible that she confided in Yossi and that he convinced her that her aunt was wrong."

"But then wouldn't she have gone away with him? Why would he still be hanging around L.A.?"

"True. And he did have those plane tickets to Israel that they never used. Still, I want to talk to him again."

"Call him."

"I will. In a minute." I snuggled up to my husband again. "I missed you."

"I missed you, too," he said, kissing me. Suddenly, thirty pounds of outrage landed in our laps.

"Hey! Stop it!" Ruby shouted, wriggling her way in between us. She held up her face to her father. "Kiss me instead!"

Peter kissed her on the nose. "You know, I'm allowed to kiss *both* my girls." He leaned over the top of her head and kissed my nose, too.

Ruby placed a hand on either side of his face and kissed him, over and over again. "This is *my* daddy," she said.

"Okay, Baby Electra." I hoisted myself off the couch. "I'm going to make some phone calls."

Yossi was home when I called. When I told him I had news about Fraydle he agreed to let me come over. I left Peter with the kids and headed out the door. I considered the nightmare of parking on Melrose Avenue—especially on the weekend when all the kids from the Valley pour into the city in their SUVs to buy platform shoes and artfully torn jeans and get their tongues, lips, navels, and other parts punctured—and decided to walk the half-mile or so to Yossi's house.

Without my stroller or a jogging suit as an excuse, I stuck out like a sore thumb as I marched up La Brea. I walked by Nettie's store without even glancing in and made it to Melrose in no time at all. It was a bit tougher going on the trendy avenue itself, as I had to keep dodging giggling clumps of teenage girls and whizzing herds of skateboarders. After staring at what seemed like three million bared midriffs, I had just about decided that I was the fattest person in the Los Angeles basin when two Harley Davidsons roared by, piloted by a pair of massive women with long hair streaming out of tiny pink helmets. Who knew they made leather clothes that big?

Those women obviously looked and felt gorgeous. There they were, tricked out in their leather pants, squealing down Melrose Avenue, wordlessly shouting, *We're here, we're gigantic, get used to it!* And there I was, a few pounds overweight, skulking down the same avenue, wordlessly shouting, *I'm fat, I'm ugly, ignore me!* What was wrong with this picture? I had a husband who loved

me—belly, thighs, and all. My body had just produced and
was giving sustenance to a big, healthy baby boy. Why
wasn't I able to feel better about myself?

I thought about my little daughter, with her gorgeous
potbelly and lovely soft skin. If I didn't get over this obsession with my weight, and soon, my contagion would
spread to her. The last thing I wanted was for her to be one
of those pathetic eight-year-olds, complaining about their
weight and guzzling Diet Coke.

In the midst of this reverie, I arrived at Yossi's building.
I walked into the courtyard which, on that sunny Sunday
afternoon, was populated with the tenants of the apartments, lounging in their deck chairs and sitting on the edge
of the fountain. Rap music blared from a speaker propped
in an open window. Yossi's door was open and he stood in
the doorway, leaning against the doorjamb. He was smok-
ing a cigarette and wearing a flannel shirt with the sleeves
cut off. His feet were bare and his jeans looked at though
they hadn't been washed in a while.

I walked across the courtyard, followed by the curious
gazes of his neighbors. At thirty-three I was probably the
oldest person there. Yossi lifted his hand in a halfhearted
gesture of welcome and, with a nod at me to follow, turned
back into his apartment. I walked in and shut the door behind me.

The entire apartment was one large room, with a kitchenette at one end.

"Please, sit down," Yossi said, pointing at a futon-bed
covered with an unsavory looking Indian print bedspread.
"Can I get you some coffee? All I have is café *botz*."

"*Botz*?" I asked, perching on the very edge of the bed.

"Mud. Like Turkish coffee. In Hebrew we call it mud
coffee."

Delicious. "Oh. Sure, mud sounds great."

He walked into the little kitchenette, and I watched as he scooped what I looked more like dirt than mud into two coffee mugs and poured in boiling water. He added two heaping teaspoons of sugar to each cup and gave them a brisk stir. Handing me my mug, he said, "Let it sit for a minute so your mouth doesn't get full of grounds."

Even more delicious.

He pulled a folding chair away from the card table that stood against the far wall of the room and sat down backwards in the chair, his legs straddling the seat and his arms leaning on the back.

"Did you find Fraydle?" he asked.

"No, I didn't find her. I did find out some things, though."

"What? What did you find out?"

"I found out that she was going to marry Ari Hirsch."

"I told you that," he said. "I told you that she decided to be a good girl and do what her father told her."

"I also found out that Ari Hirsch may be gay."

"Gay? Like a *faygeleh*?"

I winced. "Gay like homosexual, yes." I took a sip of the hot, sweet coffee. It *was* delicious.

"She can't marry him now! She'll never marry him when she hears about this!" he crowed.

"She knows."

"What do you mean? She knows? But you said you didn't find her. Did she find out before? Oh my God, is that why she is gone? Did she find out about him and he did something to her?"

"I don't know, Yossi. But I don't think so. Ari says that they discussed it and decided to go forward with the marriage, anyway."

"What are you talking about? That is ridiculous." He stood up and pushed the chair away. It fell to the floor with a crash and he angrily righted it. "Why would she marry a *faygeleh*? She would not want a pretend marriage—a life without sex."

"I don't know, Yossi. Maybe she thought that once Ari was married he would change. I take it that you don't know anything about this. Fraydle never told you about Ari?"

"No! Of course not! If I knew about this do you think she would be missing? I would never have let her go forward with this marriage. I would have taken her away!" He seemed to realize what he had just said. "I didn't do anything!" he bellowed, and then let loose a stream of Hebrew.

Suddenly, he rushed over to me. "You!" he said, grabbing my arm and dragging me roughly to my feet. "I don't need you here in my house, accusing me of this. You get out! Get out!" He shoved me toward the door. I scooped up my purse with one hand and shook off his arm with the other.

"I'm leaving," I said, in as dignified a tone as I could muster. "I'm not accusing you of anything, Yossi. I'm just trying to get to the bottom of this. All I want is to find Fraydle. Isn't that what you want, too?" He looked at me angrily, and then his shoulders sagged and he slumped, defeated.

"Yes," he whispered.

"I'm going now."

He nodded and let go of my arm.

"You have my number, right?"

He nodded again.

"You'll call me if you hear anything."

He nodded a third time.

I strode out the door and shut it firmly behind me. I

stood in the courtyard for a minute, taking a breath to quiet my racing heart. I sure was getting good at pissing people off. Oh, let's be honest; I've always possessed that particular quality in spades.

A voice rang out from above. "Hello! Juliet!"

I looked up, and saw Anat, the waitress from Nomi's. She waved at me and shouted, "One minute! I'll come down."

She ran down the stairs.

"Have you found her? Yossi's girlfriend?"

"No." I shook my head. I glanced back to Yossi's door to make sure it was still closed. "Anat, did you remember anything more about her, about them?" I asked, not particularly hopefully.

"Maybe," she said, in a conspiratorial whisper. "You want to get a cup of coffee? We can talk."

I hadn't actually managed to have more than a sip of the mud Yossi had prepared for me, and I needed a shot of caffeine.

"Is there somewhere we can go?"

"For coffee? On Melrose?" she asked, incredulous. We walked out of the courtyard. It took us a minute or two to choose which of the seven coffee shops on the block we would find the most comfortable.

We settled for a Starbucks on the opposite side of the street. "It'll be more private," Anat said. "None of the people on the courtyard buy coffee there."

We walked into the café and up to the counter. I ordered a mochaccino, which I once heard has the calories of a milk shake. I dumped in a rather ludicrous packet of Equal and shook an inch-thick layer of chocolate flakes onto the top of the foam. Anat got a triple espresso. No wonder she looked so thin. And wired.

We made our way over to a couple of comfortable arm-chairs and sat down. Say what you will about the Starbucks-ing of America, the stores sure are cozy. And, I've always liked the somewhat watery brew. I like a cup of coffee I can sip, not chew. Except for the chocolate flakes.

"I've been thinking about the last time I saw Yossi's girl-friend," Anat said to me. She was obviously relishing the prospect of gossiping about her ex. "Maybe two weeks ago, maybe a little less, I saw her here one day after the next. Both times she was upset."

"Upset?"

"The first time, she looked furious. I noticed her because she slammed his door so hard that I came out of my apart-ment. She was pale, like a sheet. But you know, she still looked beautiful. Like a movie star. Those big eyes."

"And then you saw her again?"

Anat sipped daintily at her espresso. I gulped my frothy, fat-filled festival of chocolate. "Yes," she said. "She came back the next morning. I was sitting out on the balcony and I saw her run into the courtyard. Something was wrong. She looked terrible. She knocked on his door and when he answered it she pushed into the apartment. It was like he didn't want to let her in, but she pushed by him. I waited on the balcony, watching, and then maybe ten minutes later, she flew out. This time she was crying hysterically. She ran out of the courtyard. And that was the last time I saw her."

"Could she have come back when you weren't around?"

"It's possible, but I asked the others and nobody saw her there, either. A lot of us noticed her when she made those two dramatic exits, but nobody I talked to saw her come back again. If she did, it was when none of us were home."

I leaned back in my chair. Yossi had told me that they'd argued, but he certainly hadn't told me that she'd left him once in a rage and once weeping. This seemed like information critical to Fraydle's disappearance. I realized that Anat wasn't the most reputable of witnesses. She herself had a motive to do away with Fraydle. She was obviously still in love with Yossi. Nobody is that interested in an old boyfriend unless she still cares.

By now I was convinced that something very bad had happened to Fraydle. It was time to tell Fraydle's parents about this. And it was time to call the police.

Twenty-two

"I told you, Juliet, if they hear nothing by *Shabbos*, Sima will insist they go to the police. Before that, I can do nothing."

I leaned on the counter at the front of Nettie's market, where I had rushed immediately after leaving Starbucks.

"Listen, Nettie, I don't think Fraydle ran away. I think that something has happened to her. Friday is too long to wait. By then, it might be too late."

Nettie drew back, anxiously knotting a cloth in her hands. She shook her head. "I can do nothing. Nothing."

"Nettie, Fraydle had a boyfriend. An Israeli boyfriend. Not religious. I'm afraid he might have hurt her because she was getting married."

Nettie shook her head furiously. "What are you talking? A boyfriend. That's ridiculous."

"She went to his apartment. I talked to him, I talked to his neighbors."

Nettie gasped, "*Mein Gott.*"

"It's time to go to the police."

She nodded. "You go talk to Sima." She glanced around the store as if looking for something. "Listen, this is what you'll do. I'll call her and tell her I'm sending you to get something from the garage. And then when you go get the box, you'll talk to her."

"What?" I asked, confused.

"I use her garage for storage. My storage area is so small and they have lots of room. It's their *Pesach* kitchen, their kosher-for-Passover kitchen, and during the rest of the year they don't use it. So I put my things there. I'll tell her I need a box from the garage, and while you're there, you'll talk to her."

"Nettie, I'll just go over to talk to her. I don't need an excuse."

Nettie shook her head. "She's not going to talk to you. She won't even let you in the house. Baruch told her not to talk to you anymore."

"What? Why?"

Nettie shrugged her shoulders. She picked up the phone and dialed.

"Listen, Sima, I'm sending someone over to pick up a case of"—her eyes scanned the empty shelves—"a case of tuna fish. I'm out. I can't come myself because the store is full of customers. They won't leave me alone today." She gestured wildly around the empty shop and hung up the phone.

I rolled my eyes at this unnecessary subterfuge. Nettie obviously didn't want to be there while I coerced Sima into going to the police. I walked quickly out the back door, down the alley, and to the Finkelstein house. Fraydle's younger brothers were once again playing on the porch. I climbed the steps, smiled reassuringly at them, and knocked on the door.

Fraydle's mother came to the door. When she saw me, she began to shake her head.

"Please," I said. "I just need to get a case of tuna for Nettie."

Sima looked at me for a minute, and then shrugged her shoulders. "Come," she said, leading me into the house and to the kitchen. The little boys trailed after us. I stood awkwardly for a moment and watched as one of the youngsters crawled onto a kitchen chair. He reached out for the sugar bowl sitting in the middle of the table and sent it flying to the ground, shattering in an explosion of sugar and porcelain. Remembering Sarah and the broken saucer, I flinched. Sima, however, didn't react the way I'd expected her to. She merely kissed the top of the boy's head, and reached for a broom and a dustpan to sweep up the fragments and spilled crystals.

"The garage is down those stairs." She pointed toward a door in the wall next to the stove. I opened the door and walked down the steep wooden stairs into the gloom of the garage. There was a rickety banister that I didn't dare touch for fear it wouldn't support even the weight of my hand. The garage was entirely taken up by boxes piled against walls and by a complete kitchen set up in one corner. There was a small stove, an old refrigerator, a metal sink, and an ancient chest freezer.

I walked toward the piled-up boxes and began searching for a case of tuna. A low hum filled the garage. I lifted my head and looked around. The hum seemed to be coming from the freezer. I walked over and put my hand on the top. It was cold. This was, Nettie had said, the Passover kitchen. The holiday wasn't for months. I heard my grandmother's voice in my mind, "*Aroysgevorfen* electricity!" A waste of electricity. My mouth grew dry. I grasped the handles of the freezer and gave a tug. With a hiss, the top lifted up, and I screamed.

Fraydle looked as though she were asleep, except she was very white. She was curled up in the freezer, with her legs up against her chest. Her eyes were open just a crack, enough to see that they had rolled back in her head. Frost crystals had formed over her eyes and mouth. Her head rested in a pool of something frozen and black. Blood.

Suddenly I became aware of the thumping noise of footsteps coming down the stairs. I dropped the lid of the freezer and backed away from it.

Sima rushed down the stairs, the little boys close behind her. When she saw me she stopped dead in her tracks. "What? What?" she asked, her face pale. Her hands reached out and grabbed the boys by their collars, not allowing them to cross the floor toward me. Sima stood motionless, her white knuckles gripping the backs of her sons' shirts as they wriggled, trying to escape her grasp. She looked into my face.

"Fraydle?" she whispered.

"Yes."

"Where?"

I looked at the freezer and she moaned. She knelt down and scooped the little boys into her arms, burying her face in their necks. Great, rasping sobs shook her body, and the boys grew silent and pale at the sight of their mother's tears. I stood there with the wailing woman and her children for what felt like hours, but was surely not more than a moment or two. Then I led them up the stairs to the kitchen and shut the door at the top of the stairs behind me. I sat them at the table, lifted the phone, and, finally, many days after I should have, dialed 911.

Twenty-three

BY the time they let me go home, I had leaked though my breast pads and soaked my shirt. It was only the sight of me dripping all over myself that convinced the police officers to allow me to leave. Before I made my escape, a detective interviewed me in the little room where I'd nursed Isaac the first time I was at Fraydle's house. I told the investigating officer, a woman of about my age with close-cropped brown hair and horn-rimmed glasses, everything I knew, including Yossi's name and address. I even disclosed Ari's sexual orientation. At this point I knew I could hold nothing back. The police needed to know everything so that they could find out who had done this horrible thing.

I walked the few blocks from the Finkelsteins' house to my own quickly, desperate to see my husband and kids. My eyes were dry, which surprised me, as I'm a woman who can be reduced to tears by a television commercial. I hadn't cried once since we'd discovered Fraydle's body. It was as if I couldn't lay claim to tears in the presence of Sima and the rabbi, who had walked into the horror on the heels of the police. Their mourning was so complete and total that my tears would have been a pale and inappropriate shadow.

The scene I left behind me in Sima's kitchen was quiet and miserable. Fraydle's father leaned against the counter, his body folded and almost shrunken in despair. Nettie, whom I'd called after I'd spoken to the police, and Sima sat at the kitchen table, each kneading a dishtowel and, periodically, using it to wipe their streaming eyes or noses. Fraydle's littlest brothers were huddled in a corner of the kitchen. Sarah sat in a chair next to her mother, shaking and weeping, gripping Sima's hand in her own. The older boys stood around the edges of the room, eyes wet with tears and faces pale.

When I reached my house, I unlocked the door and ran up the stairs into my apartment. I found Peter in the rocking chair, feeding Isaac a bottle. Ruby was watching television.

"Juliet! Where have you been? It's been almost four hours! I was completely freaking out!" Peter shouted.

I ran across the room and, kneeling beside his chair, put my head in his lap next to Isaac's warm body. The baby spat out the bottle nipple, grasped a piece of my hair in his little fist and shoved it into his mouth. Only then did I start to cry.

Peter stroked my hair with his hand. "What happened, honey? What happened? Are you okay?"

I hiccupped and sat up. I looked over at Ruby, who was so enraptured by the dancing purple dinosaur on TV that she had not even noticed my tears.

"Fraydle's dead," I whispered.

Peter didn't look surprised. "I was afraid of that," he murmured. "How?"

"I don't know. Peter, I found her body." I was still whispering.

He looked at me, his mouth open and his eyes wide.

I told him about how I had found poor Fraydle shoved into the freezer.

"What's a Passover kitchen?" he interrupted at that point in my story.

"At Passover you can't eat any bread, only matzo. Really strict Orthodox won't even cook in the same kitchen that bread was ever prepared in. So they keep an entirely separate kitchen to do their Passover cooking. They never let anything that's not kosher for Passover into that kitchen so that it will never be spoiled."

"Oh," he said. The two of us were silent for a moment, thinking about the horrible despoiling of the Finkelsteins' kosher kitchen.

I continued: "When I was in the garage, I heard the freezer humming. It didn't make sense that there would be something in the freezer, because Passover is still months away. I just walked over and opened it." My eyes filled with tears again.

"Hey! Why are you crying?" Ruby shouted. She had momentarily looked up from Barney.

I quickly wiped my eyes. "It's nothing, honey. I'm just tired." I turned to Peter. "What's the baby drinking?" I asked.

"Formula."

"What?"

"Juliet, you weren't here and he was going nuts. There

wasn't any breast milk in the freezer. I found that sample can of formula that they gave us at the hospital. He seems to like it fine."

I shrugged my shoulders, too exhausted by the events of the afternoon to argue. Also, I realized that I couldn't expect Peter to share my obsession with keeping my nursing infant pure of the contamination of baby formula. I wasn't really sure, myself, why I felt so strongly about it. I took the baby from Peter's arms and nestled him in my lap on the couch. He rooted madly as I freed a breast for him. He gave a contented sigh as he latched on.

"Oh, I almost forgot," Peter said. "You got a message from Barbara Rosen."

"Who?" I asked. "I don't know anyone named Barbara Rosen."

"She said she's Jake's mother."

"Jake who?" I asked.

"Jake Rosen, I assume."

"I don't know any Jake or Barbara Rosen."

"Mama!" Ruby shouted. "Jake in my class!"

"Oh, right. Jake's mommy. What did she want?"

"She said she just called to remind you that *The Boys From Syracuse* is tomorrow afternoon."

I'd forgotten all about our plan. "Oh, right. Her older son's play. She thought it would be fun if we took the kids to see it."

"I wanna go, Mama!" Ruby said.

"Okay, honey," I said, thinking that sitting through a children's production of a Rodgers and Hart musical was a little more than I could handle right at that moment.

"I wrote down all the details," Peter said. "She'll save seats for you and Ruby."

"Do you want to go instead?" I asked hopefully.

"Do you need me to go?" Peter asked.

"No, I guess not."

"Good, because I'd rather have root canal. But have fun."

THE police came by again later that day. The female detective who'd spoken to me at Fraydle's house was accompanied by an older man in an ill-fitting navy suit with the unmistakable sheen of polyester. She introduced her partner, Carl Hopkins, and herself, Susan Black.

Peter took the kids out to play in the yard and I sat at the kitchen table, hands wrapped around a steaming cup of chamomile tea and, once again, and in more detail, told the officers everything I knew about Fraydle's death.

"How well did you know the victim?" asked Detective Black.

"Not well at all. She baby-sat for me once, and then didn't show up the next day. When I went looking for her, that's when I found out that she was gone."

"And when was that?"

"A little over a week ago."

"And why didn't you call the police then?" Detective Hopkins interrupted.

I turned to him. "It wasn't my place to. I couldn't report her as a missing person. Only her parents could have done that."

"That's not exactly true, ma'am," Detective Black said. "You couldn't have filed a report, because we would need a member of the family to verify that the girl was actually missing, but you certainly could have alerted us to her absence."

I nodded my head and softly said, "I could have, and in retrospect I should have."

Once we'd gone over the details of my search for Fraydle, Detective Black gave me her card and asked me to call her if I heard anything new. Then she leaned back in her chair, looked at me intently for a moment, and said, "Ms. Applebaum, I used to work with Detective Mitch Carswell of the Santa Monica Police Department."

I swallowed, not a little nervously.

"I understand that you were helpful to him in solving the Hathaway murder."

Helpful? If single-handedly finding out who killed Abigail Hathaway, the headmistress of Los Angeles's most selective nursery school, qualifies as helpful, then I suppose I was.

"Yes," I said.

"I understand that you were shot by Ms. Hathaway's killer."

I looked into Detective Black's face. Her expression was absolutely impassive.

"Yes," I said.

"Ms. Applebaum, we at the Los Angeles Police Department take our work very seriously." She paused, as if waiting for me to say something. I didn't. I just looked at her. Detective Hopkins stared at me balefully.

Finally, Detective Black continued. "This is *my* homicide investigation, Ms. Applebaum. I am the primary detective on the case. I expect you to provide me with any and all information you possess."

"As I have," I said.

She held up her hand as if to still my voice. "And I expect that you will do nothing else. No more trips to New York. No more interviews with witnesses. Nothing. Do you understand?"

I considered defending myself and explaining to her exactly why I'd investigated Fraydle's disappearance, but decided it wasn't worth the effort. I wasn't going to convince the two detectives that they needed the services of a crime-solving soccer-mom-in-training to track down Fraydle's killer. All the same, I felt a niggling sense of irritation. Why couldn't the woman just say thank you and assure me that she would competently carry out the investigation? Why did she feel the need to warn me off, as if I were some recalcitrant adolescent mucking up her turf?

I nodded my head once, and rose from my chair. "If there's nothing else, Detective, I'd like to get back to my husband and children," I said.

"Do you understand me, Ms. Applebaum?" Detective Black asked again, also rising from her seat.

"Of course, Detective. Let me see you and your associate out."

I hustled the two of them out the door, then turned and walked through the apartment to Peter's office, at the back of the house. Leaning out the window overlooking the back yard, I shouted "All clear." As my family came clomping up the back stairs, I looked around Peter's office. Every available shelf was covered with toys. Action figures, mostly vintage and all in near-perfect condition. Peter, an avid collector, was in for a rude awakening. Ruby had never paid Peter's toys the slightest attention, but at some time in the near future Isaac was surely going to wake up to the bounty in Daddy's office and tear that Major Matt Mason right out of its original 1969 blister pack.

Twenty-four

I decided to studiously ignore the police detective's instructions and make some phone calls. I had promised both Ari and Yossi that I would let them know if I heard anything definitive about Fraydle. Her death was something pretty definite. I had my suspicions about Yossi, but I was fairly convinced that Ari was innocent of the murder. I couldn't say the same about his uncles, however. I managed to find Ari at the yeshiva, and as gently as I could, I told him about his fiancée's death. He was shocked into silence for a few moments. Finally, he spoke, "Perhaps this is a message to me."

"Excuse me?" I said.

"Perhaps *Ha Shem* is sending me a message that I should not be a married man."

"Ari," I said, "I don't think God is sending you any kind of message. What I think is that some evil person killed

Fraydle. I also think that you had better be prepared to tell the police everything."

Ari didn't seem surprised that I'd ratted him out to the cops. On the contrary, he insisted that he wanted to help in any way that he could and asked me for the detective's phone number so that he could call her right away. I had a sense that I didn't need to worry about this young man. While confused, he seemed to have a deep sense of right and wrong. He was not only able but willing to take responsibility for his own actions. I had no idea what path he would choose, but I felt that he would ultimately lead a life he could be proud of.

I couldn't get through to Yossi, and decided to call Al Hockey instead, to give him an update. His wife told me that he was out at the municipal golf course but gave me his cell phone number.

"Hockey!" he bellowed, by way of hello.

"Hi, Al, it's Juliet."

"Juliet? What the hell are you doing calling me on the golf course? Are you trying to ruin my swing?"

I could always count on Al's bluster to improve my mood. I told him about Fraydle's death and my part in the discovery of her body.

"Want me to make some calls, see what I can find out?" he asked.

"That would be great," I said. "I have a feeling the cops aren't going to be particularly forthcoming with details of their investigation." I recounted my experience with Detective Black.

"I know the woman. She's a real ball-buster."

"Al," I said, warningly. The guy was anything but politically correct.

"Hey, don't get your panties in a twist. All I meant was

that the two of you have a lot in common. I'll call you later." He hung up.

AL called within an hour and offered to come over after dinner and tell me the little he'd found out. I was surprised at his willingness to drive all the way from Westminister, the small city on the way to Orange County that he called home, to my house in Hancock Park, but I was happy at the thought of seeing him in the flesh. It had been a while.

When he arrived, my old investigator and my husband greeted one another a little uncomfortably. It wasn't that they didn't like each other. It was just that they were two different species. Al didn't know quite what to make of my nerdy husband with the shaggy hair and sensitive-guy glasses who made his living writing movies about cannibals, homicidal androids, and teenage succubae. Peter hadn't spent much time around middle-aged men with brush cuts and Marine Corps tattoos whose libraries contained pirated copies of the Zapruder tape and books with titles like *The Trilateral Commission Exposed*. The two men shook hands and made a few awkward comments about the Dodgers' chances next season. Whatever would men talk about if it weren't for sports?

Turning to me, Al said, "So where are those kids of yours?"

"Ruby's asleep, or at least in bed. Isaac's over there in his Johnny-Jump-Up.

"Johnny-what-up?" Al said.

"You know, that jumpy thing. Haven't you ever seen one of those? It's a kind of harness that hooks in a doorway and lets the baby jump up and down. He'll stay quiet in there for hours."

As if to illustrate my point, Isaac sprang up and down a few times and laughed.

"Interesting contraption," Al said, walking over to Isaac.

"You know," I told him, "if you'd let your daughters get married, you might have a grandchild to buy one of those contraptions for." Al was legendary for driving away potential mates for his three girls, all of whom still lived at home although they were well into their twenties.

"Yeah, well, soon as one of 'em brings home a man instead of a degenerate pile a crap, excuse my French, I'll be slapping down my checkbook for a caterer and a band. But honestly, Juliet, you should see these guys. Earrings. Nose rings. *Nipple* rings, for crying out loud!"

Peter self-consciously covered his pierced left earlobe. "Um, honey, I'd better get to work, if you don't mind," he said.

"Sure, babe. Hey, Peter, why don't you show Al your bellybutton stud!"

Al blanched and Peter rolled his eyes. "I do *not* have a stud in my bellybutton. Very funny, Juliet." He walked out of the room.

"Does he?" Al asked, obviously horrified.

I smiled mysteriously.

Suddenly, I remembered why he was there. "I can't believe we're sitting here joking around. Tell me what you found out about Fraydle's death."

Al plopped himself down on the couch and swung his feet onto the coffee table.

"Make yourself comfortable. Can I get you something to drink? Coffee? Tea?"

"Tea?" he asked, incredulous. "How about a beer? Something American."

"I'll check." Rooting around in the fridge, I managed to locate an ancient bottle of Sam Adams from a party we'd had no more than a year before. I popped the top off and brought the bottle out to Al. "How's this?" I asked.

He took a long swallow, burped, and said, "Fine."

"What did you turn up?" I sat down in an armchair opposite him. I glanced over at Isaac, who was contentedly gnawing on one of the hanging straps holding him in the air.

"I talked to Fat Rolly Rollins, a detective in the division that includes Hancock Park. He's an old buddy. Obviously they have no official cause of death yet, but the M. E. on the scene said the girl had a broken neck. She also suffered some kind of blow to her head."

"Which of those killed her?" I asked.

"No way for them to tell now, although Fat Rolly did say it looks like she could have died by falling down the stairs and hitting her head on the concrete floor."

"Falling down the stairs? And then what? Conveniently landing in the freezer, which then plugged itself in?"

"Maybe she was pushed."

"Could someone have hit her on the head?"

"I suppose so. All I can tell you is what Fat Rolly heard from the officers on the scene. The M.E. said it looked like a fall to him."

"Okay, what about time of death? Did the medical examiner have an estimate?"

"Not even a tentative at the scene. He couldn't guess at anything, because of the freezer."

"Did Fat Freddy—"

"Rolly. Fat Rolly."

"Did Fat Rolly tell you if they had any suspects?"

"No, but Juliet, in cases like this they look to the family."

I knew that. Most murder victims die at the hands of someone they know, and the circumstances of Fraydle's death seemed to point particularly to the members of her family. Her body had been found at home. Her parents had failed to notify the police of her disappearance. It certainly looked damning.

I told Al about Ari and his uncles and filled him in on my latest experiences with Yossi.

"So what do you want to do now?" Al asked.

"I don't know. Nothing, I guess."

"Yeah, right."

"No, really. I'm going to let the police figure this out."

Al snorted. "Whatever you say, Detective. I'd better get going. I'm going to be late."

"Late? Where are you going?"

"You think I drove all the way to this cesspool of a city just to see you?" Al asked. "No way. I've got a meeting."

"What meeting?"

"Southern L.A. Basin Chapter of the Freedom Brigade," he said proudly.

"A militia! Are you out of your mind?"

"Listen, missy, last time I checked, the Constitution of this great nation still guaranteed us the right to a well-regulated militia. I'm just doing my bit to keep that alive."

How could such a warm, loving guy with such an astute investigative mind be such a nut case?

"Just promise me that you're not a white supremacist, Al," I said.

He gave me a disgusted look. "Juliet, have you ever seen my wife?"

I thought for a moment. "No, I don't think I have."

"But you've seen pictures of my kids, right?"

"Of course." Al's office was covered with pictures of his three, dark-haired, beautiful daughters.

"Ever notice that my girls are biracial?"

"What? Really?" I hadn't.

"My wife's African-American, Juliet."

I blushed. "Oh, wow. I'm sorry about the white supremacist comment."

"Whatever. Us freedom fighters, we have to deal with that kind of ignorant nonsense all the time. Just because we don't swallow every word the federal government says doesn't mean we're a bunch of racists. I'll have you know that my chapter is full of all kinds. Black, white, Asian, Latino, you name it."

I was just about to comment on how nice it was that his particular department of the lunatic fringe was an equal opportunity employer when I decided to give it up. You just can't win with Al. Every time I wind up in one of those conversations with him, I swear to myself I'm never again going to mention Roswell, David Koresh, or the United Nations.

I got up and gave Al a kiss on the cheek. "Thanks for the information, Al. I really appreciate it."

He blushed. "No problem, girlie. I'll talk to you." He hoisted himself out of the couch and left.

Twenty-five

TRUE to her promise, Barbara Rosen had saved us seats at the performance of *The Boys From Syracuse*. Ruby and Jake sat next to each other, holding hands and giggling. I settled Isaac in my lap and tried to nurse him to sleep, much to Barbara's horror. Apparently, baring the breast, even under cover of a shirt and a draped baby blanket, is just not done at the better Los Angeles private schools. What could I do? It was either get the kid to sleep, or listen to him cry through the entire performance.

While the baby nursed, and Barbara tried very hard to look as if she was not utterly humiliated to be seen with us, I checked out the mobbed auditorium. The attendees were mostly mommies, although there were a number of daddies who'd managed to escape from the office. Virtually all the daddies were watching the play through the eyepiece of their video cameras. Every second person was holding a bouquet of flowers, as if this were opening night at the opera rather than a junior high school production. The smell of roses was thick and heady.

The lights dimmed and the orchestra struck up an almost recognizable version of the play's overture. I looked down at Isaac, who had thankfully dropped off to sleep, and settled back in my chair, determined to try to enjoy the show.

It actually wasn't awful. The sets and costumes were almost professional, and there were some hysterical moments when the young boy playing the duke took off his hat with a flourish, inadvertently releasing into the air huge clouds of the baby powder that had been used to whiten his hair. I even found myself humming along to the songs. It was in Act I, as I was tapping my feet to "This Can't Be Love," that I began to get the beginnings of an idea. As I watched the preadolescent Dromios get hit over the head and an Adriana in braces drag home the wrong Antipholus, it became clearer in my mind. By the time Dromios shrieked, with a rather endearing lisp, "Shakespeare!" I knew who had murdered Fraydle.

I sat through a full twenty minutes of standing ovations before I could finally bear it no longer. I whispered a hurried goodbye to Barbara and Jake and, carrying Isaac and dragging an unwilling Ruby, ran out to the car.

"But I don't want to leave!" Ruby wailed, as I buckled her into her car seat.

"I'm sorry, honey," I said. "But the play is over and Mama has an errand to run."

I drove much too quickly down Santa Monica Boulevard, dialing Peter's cell phone as I whipped through yellow lights. I reached his voice mail. Cursing, I tried his assistant. Voice mail again. I wasn't going to be able to unload Ruby and Isaac. I turned onto Melrose Avenue and drove to Nomi's restaurant. I parked in the last spot in the lot, yanked the kids out of the car, and hustled them into the almost-empty restaurant. Anat sat at a table, reading a Hebrew newspaper.

"Hi! What's going on?" she asked.

"Anat, I have a question for you. You told me that the last time you saw Fraydle she looked weird. What did you mean by that?"

She shrugged and wrinkled her brow. "I can't explain it. She just looked different."

I leaned forward and looked at her intently. "Could you have seen someone else, someone who looked like Fraydle, but wasn't Fraydle?"

Anat looked at me, puzzled. "I don't think so. It was her. Same hair, same clothes. She just looked—I dunno, different."

"Like less pretty?"

"Exactly!"

"Could it have been someone who looked like Fraydle, but wasn't as pretty?"

Anat looked skeptical. "I guess so," she said, not sounding particularly confident.

I thanked her, gathered up the kids and ran out the door of the restaurant to the car. I buckled them into their car seats for the millionth time that day, and headed back up Santa Monica Boulevard. As I drove, I thought once more about Anat. The fact that Fraydle's body had been found in her own parents' home seemed to rule Anat out as a suspect. I couldn't imagine the Hasidic girl inviting Anat into her house. And besides, I knew who killed Fraydle. I just needed someone to tell me why.

I pulled into the Gap parking lot and jumped out of the

car. I stuck Isaac in his stroller and convinced Ruby to postpone her tantrum with the promise of an ice cream reward. I didn't even bother to pretend to be visiting the store, but just walked right up the block into the courtyard of Yossi's apartment building and knocked on the door. After a few moments it opened a crack. Yossi grimaced when he saw me and tried to close the door in my face.

"Yossi!" I said. "You have to talk to me. Please. I know what happened with Fraydle."

Now, I didn't *know* anything. I merely suspected. However, I was sure that the only way to get Yossi to tell me the truth was to pretend that I already knew it.

He opened the door slowly. His face was unshaven and he looked pale and ill. I pointed to Isaac, who was sitting in his stroller chewing on his fist, and to Ruby, who was throwing sticks and pebbles into the fountain.

"I have my children with me," I said. "Let's sit out here so I can watch them."

He looked at me for a moment, and then walked out of his apartment and sank into one of the two lawn chairs in front of his door. I perched on the other one and made sure that Ruby was far enough away that she couldn't hear our conversation.

I sat silently for a minute, and then I said softly, "You were sleeping with Fraydle's sister, Sarah."

He didn't deny it. He didn't even look surprised. He simply said, in a hoarse whisper, "Has she told the police?"

"I don't know," I answered.

He looked up at me. "I didn't kill Fraydle. I loved her. I still love her."

I nodded. "Tell me what happened, Yossi."

"It was after Fraydle told me about Ari Hirsch. She came one day and we were together, like always. Then, afterwards, she kissed me and said goodbye. She said she had to marry Ari, that her father insisted and that it was important to the whole family. She said her father needed the alliance with the Hirsch family. She told me she loved me but that she had to take care of her family."

His eyes filled with tears.

"Go on," I murmured.

"I begged her not to leave me. I promised her that I would take care of her family. I even promised to *chozer b'tshuvah*, to become Hasidic. She wouldn't listen. She just said that it had already been decided. She had accepted him. And then she left. She just got up and left.

"For days I tried to talk to her. I looked for her at the store. I walked up and down the streets looking for her. I couldn't find her anywhere. It was like she had disappeared. Finally, one day, I saw her sister, Sarah, walking home from school. I stopped her and begged her to take a message to Fraydle. She said she knew all about Fraydle and me. She said she knew we'd been together, that she'd followed Fraydle to my house. She promised to help me, to talk to Fraydle for me. She told me to wait at my house and that she would come to me after she'd talked to Fraydle.

"Sarah came that evening, right before dark. She sat down on my couch and told me that Fraydle didn't love me. She said that Fraydle wanted to move to New York, that she wanted to be with Ari Hirsch. Sarah said that Fraydle told her she was tired of me and was glad of the excuse not to be with me anymore.

"I didn't know what to say. I just sat there, in shock. And then Sarah came over to me, and kissed me. She kissed me, and she took off her clothes and . . . and . . . "

"And you slept with her," I said.

He nodded. "She looks so much like Fraydle," he whispered. "I closed my eyes and it was like being with Fraydle." He paused. "Look, I know it was terrible. I know it was unforgivable, but you have to understand, Fraydle had left me and I needed her so much."

I couldn't give him the absolution he craved. "Did you see Sarah again?"

"No, I mean, I saw her but we didn't—we weren't together again."

"What happened?"

"After she left, I just went to sleep. I woke up the next day to someone banging on my door. It was Fraydle. She came into the room and she was smiling. She looked so happy! But then she saw Sarah's sweater. Sarah had left her sweater on the chair. Fraydle stopped talking and picked up the sweater. She looked confused and asked me what it was doing there. I lied to her. I told her that it was hers, that she'd left it there, but she shook her head. And then she looked at the bed."

"The bed?" I asked.

"I woke up to answer the door. The bed wasn't made. She saw . . . the blood."

"Sarah was a virgin."

He nodded.

"What did Fraydle do?"

"She picked up the sweater and she walked out the door. She slammed it so hard, plaster fell from the ceiling."

"Did you follow her?" I asked.

"No." He shook his head. "I didn't know what to say to her. I was so ashamed."

"What did you do?"

"Nothing for a while. I just sat there. Then, I went to the travel agent and I bought the plane tickets. I wanted to prove to Fraydle that I loved only her and wanted only her.

I was sure I could convince her that I'd only been with her sister because I missed *her*, because I wanted to be with *her*. I was sure if I bought the tickets, she would understand how much I loved her and she would come with me. Come to Israel and marry me."

"Did you see Sarah again?"

"She came the next day. I went to find Fraydle in the morning. That was when you saw me outside your house. Fraydle was angry, furious at me. She said she wouldn't go with me and to leave her alone. I came back here. I just lay on the bed, trying to figure out what to do. And then Sarah showed up. She knocked on the door, and I told her to go away. She pushed her way inside. She came up to me and tried to kiss me, but I pushed her away. I just snapped. All the pressure building inside me just exploded." He looked ashamed. "I said terrible things. I told her to go away, that she disgusted me. I told her that she was a whore."

"What did she do? What did she say?"

"Nothing. She just started to cry, and ran away. That's the last time I saw her."

"Did you ever see Fraydle again?"

"No. But I think she must have wanted to come with me. I think she was going to come, and that's why she was killed." His voice rose sharply. Ruby turned around at the sound.

"It's okay, honey," I reassured her. "Mommy is just having a talk. Everything is fine."

She turned back to her game and I looked at Yossi. "Yossi, what do you think happened to Fraydle? Who do you think killed her?"

He didn't answer. Instead, he just buried his head in his hands.

"I want you to come with me to Fraydle's house," I said.

He shook his head, not bothering to lift it up.

"I want you to come with me to confront Sarah and her family. I know that your relationship with Sarah is why Fraydle died."

Yossi raised his head and then, to my surprise, agreed to come with me. I didn't trust him enough to put him in my car and, besides, I really didn't want my kids along for this ride anymore. Dragging them on an investigation was one thing. Putting them in danger was something else entirely. I told Yossi that I'd meet him at the Finkelsteins' home in an hour and bundled the kids back down the block and into the car, which, thankfully, had not yet been towed. I drove as fast as I could down Melrose Avenue, dialing Peter's number. Of course he wasn't answering. His assistant, however, picked up her phone. She told me that Peter was on his way back to the set from a meeting off the lot. When I informed her that it was an emergency, she promised to tell him that I was coming and to call the security booth so that they would let me in.

The kids and I tore through the studio lot in the direction of Sound Stage #6 where they were shooting the interiors of Peter's show. I parked in a spot clearly marked No Parking and once again unloaded my children. We walked brazenly through the Authorized Entry Only door and onto the cavernous sound stage. On the far end was a perfect replica of a 1970s-style kitchen. Ruby looked over at the stage and then let loose with a piercing shriek that brought the bustling crowd to a standstill. A remarkably lifelike corpse lay in a pool of blood on the baby-blue, vinyl-tiled floor, a hatchet lodged comfortably in its forehead.

I clamped my hand over her eyes and crushed her face to my stomach. "It's just fake, Ruby. Pretend. It's just a picture." I tried to sound jovial and reassuring, but that was made a bit difficult by the fact that fifty or sixty people had stopped dead in their tracks and were staring at me as I stood there holding a screaming toddler and pushing a stroller containing a now-wailing infant.

"Um, excuse me," I said to the room at large. "I'm looking for Peter Wyeth."

"Juliet! How wonderful to see you." I turned in the direction of the voice and found myself staring into the perfectly made-up face of the ever-lovely Marvelous Mindy Maxx.

"Peter's not here, Juliet," she said. "He's on his way back from a meeting with the special effects guys in Burbank. He's on the road, but he should be here any minute. Can I help you with something?"

I was ambivalent for a moment, but a glance at my watch decided me. "Listen, Mindy, sorry to do this. Sorry, everybody," I called out. I turned back to my husband's producing partner. "I really need to be somewhere. It's an emergency. Is Angelika around? Can I leave the kids with her?"

Mindy paused for a second, obviously mulling over my request. The various sound, film, and props folks whom I'd disturbed turned back to their work.

"Why don't you leave the kids with me? I can watch them until Peter gets here," she said.

"No, that's okay. I'll wait." I looked around for an out-of-the-way place to deposit the children and myself.

"Really, Juliet. I don't mind."

"Really, Mindy. It's fine. I'll wait." I knew I sounded hostile, but I was too distracted by what I had to do to cover up my feelings. The truth was, I *felt* hostile toward this impeccably dressed woman who was spending way more time with my husband than I was.

Mindy shrugged her shoulders and turned away. She

walked a few steps and then turned back. "We need to talk," she said.

I felt my stomach tie itself in a knot. Was this true confessions time? Was she about to tell me that she and Peter were desperately in love? Mindy took my arm and led me a few steps toward an empty corner of the sound stage. I rolled the stroller along.

"Listen, Mindy, I can't do this now. I have my kids with me. We can't have this conversation in front of my children."

"I think we can."

"Well, you're not their mother. I am."

"I *know* that, for goodness' sake. Look, Juliet, I'm not an idiot. I know what you think is going on."

"Oh, you do, do you?"

"Yes, I do. And it isn't. Nothing is going on. We work together, that's it."

"Well, pardon me for thinking that you guys are just a little more intimate than that. I've worked with plenty of people and never been so, how shall I put it? Close."

"But you've never produced a TV series. It's a totally different level of stress and time commitment. Peter and I are forced to spend fifteen hours a day together."

"Neither of you seems to be objecting."

"Because we *like* each other. Because we're friends. Don't you know how much Peter would rather be with you?"

"Look, Mindy, I don't know what you're after here. But I don't have time for this. I have something really important I need to do. And I can't do it with my kids. I need to find Peter and get the hell out of here."

"I said you should leave them with me."

"No."

"Juliet. I'm gay."

I stared at her. "What?"

"I'm gay. I'm a lesbian. You see that woman?" She pointed toward a tall athletic woman with close-cropped blond hair bent over one of the cameras. "That's my girl-friend. I'm not having an affair with your husband. I'm having an affair with *her*."

My mouth dropped open. I didn't know what to say. "God. I *am* an idiot, aren't I? I am so sorry, Mindy. I don't even know how to begin to say how sorry I am."

"You're not an idiot. You're a new mother married to an incredibly sexy man who hasn't been able to spend much time at home lately. You're normal. You were just wrong."

"That's for sure. Why didn't my lunatic husband *tell* me this?"

"I don't know. Maybe he figured it was my business. Or maybe it just never occurred to him that you would be jeal-ous. Maybe he loves you so much he can't even imagine that you'd ever think he'd cheat on you."

Suddenly I remembered where I needed to be.

"Mindy, can you really watch the kids for me? Just until Peter gets back."

"Sure. I'd love to," she said and smiled.

"Terrific." I turned to Ruby and crouched down next to her. "Hey, kiddo, are you all right?"

"Yup," she announced. "I was just surprised by the dead guy. It's okay. It's just a show. Like a comic book."

"Right. It's not real. Listen, Ruby, Mama needs to go somewhere real quick. You're going to stay here with Mindy. It'll be so fun!"

Ruby looked unconvinced.

Mindy leaned over and said, "How'd you like to go to the makeup room and have your face painted?"

Ruby nodded.

"Okay, honey. That's a great idea. Daddy will be here in a few minutes." I handed Mindy Isaac's diaper bag. "Thanks, Mindy. This is terrific of you. Just tell Peter I'll be home as soon as I can. And I'm sorry. Really."

She waved me away with a smile and walked away with the stroller. I watched them for a second, and then tore off the sound stage and leaped into my car. As I careened down Melrose Avenue, I dug in my purse for Detective Black's card. I found it and dialed the number. Voice mail. Of course. I left a message and my cell-phone number as I pulled up in front of the Finkelsteins' house.

Yossi had arrived before me and was waiting on the corner. He stood nervously, his hands shoved into his pockets. I parked my car in a commercial loading zone and together we walked toward the house. The two little boys were in their seemingly permanent position on the porch and Nettie sat on the steps, watching them. She was wearing a dark dress and a pair of fabric slippers. Her face was blotchy and pale but she smiled wanly when she saw me. The smile dried up when she saw Yossi. I marched up the steps. At my approach, the boys ran inside.

"Nettie, this is Yossi, Fraydle's boyfriend," I said.

Nettie paled and muttered something in Yiddish.

Yossi, who'd followed me, shook his head vehemently and replied in the same language.

"You speak Yiddish?" I asked him.

"My grandmother taught me," he said.

"What did Nettie say to you?"

"She says maybe I killed Fraydle. But I told her that is not true. I told her I loved Fraydle. I wanted to marry Fraydle. I would never have killed her."

Nettie turned to me. "What do you want? Why did you

bring him here?"

"Nettie, we're going to talk to Fraydle's parents. We're going to get to the bottom of this."

She shook her head.

"Nettie. Please," I said softly. She looked at me silently for a few moments, and then shrugged her shoulders. "She is dead. What else matters?"

"Finding out who killed her matters."

"That might be true. But it might also be a terrible thing to find out."

"Maybe. But don't you think we owe it to Fraydle to find out who did this to her?"

Nettie shrugged her shoulders again and stood up with a soft groan.

"Come," she said, leading the way into the house.

Twenty-six

FRAYDLE'S parents' home was full of people. The men were in the living room, standing around in small groups, most of them holding plates heaped with food. A tall candle burned on the hall table. Through the open door to the kitchen I could see the women in their accustomed place. The soft buzz of conversation stopped entirely as Yossi and I walked inside. As we entered the room I noticed a large, dark cloth covering what I assumed was a mirror over the mantel. Jewish law requires that during the seven-day period of mourning all mirrors in the house must be covered. The furniture had been moved out of the living room. Fraydle's father and the older boys sat on low chairs pushed up against the walls. Their vests and shirts were torn to signify their mourning.

As I walked in the room, Fraydle's father lifted a hand and waved me over. I walked over to him and stood quietly, waiting for him to speak. He wept openly, as did Fraydle's brothers.

"Thank you for coming," he said.

"I am so terribly sorry for your loss, Rabbi Finkelstein."

"My sister tells me that I have misjudged you, Mrs. Applebaum. She says that you have tried very hard to find out what happened to my daughter." A fresh stream of tears streaked down his reddened cheeks.

I didn't know what to say. "I just wanted to help, Rabbi. I didn't know your daughter very well, but she was a lovely girl."

At that moment, Sima came in from the kitchen. She was also weeping. She held Sarah firmly by the hand. The girl had an expression of complete panic on her face and she sank into a low chair. I followed her gaze to Yossi, who stood, head bowed, behind me.

"Rabbi, there is something I'd like to talk to you and your wife about. In private."

The rabbi looked, for a moment, as though he was going to say no. Then, with a wave of his hand, he motioned to the crowd of men and said something in Yiddish. Within two minutes the house was empty of everyone except Fraydle's family, Yossi, and me.

As the men left the house, followed by their wives, mothers, and daughters, I watched Sarah's face grow paler and paler. The only sound that came from her was the rasping of her breath.

"Rabbi Finkelstein, Mrs. Finkelstein, this is Yossi Zinger. He was a friend of Fraydle's. And of Sarah's," I said.

The rabbi looked confused. "What are you talking about? A friend?" He turned to Yossi. "Who are you? How do you know my daughters?"

Yossi stepped forward and said, in a far firmer voice

than I imagined he would be able to muster, "I was Fraydle's boyfriend, Rabbi. I wanted to marry her."

"Boyfriend? Boyfriend?" Sima interrupted. "What do
you mean? My daughter was engaged to marry Ari Hirsch.
She had no boyfriend." Sima looked at Sarah's stricken
face. "Sarahleh, what is this man talking about? Do you
know him? Did Fraydle know him? What is happening
here?"

Sarah jumped to her feet and in a quavering voice began
to talk. "It's not my fault. Fraydle went with him. She went
to his house. She told me she was with him. She was proud
of it!"

"What are you saying?" her father roared. He turned to
me. "Is this true?"

I nodded.

"And did he kill her? Did you kill my daughter?" His
shout made the walls of the house shake.

"No! I did not kill her," Yossi said. "I loved her. I wanted
to marry her."

"But she didn't want you!" Sarah wailed. "She said she
was going to marry Ari. That *Abba* and *Ema* wanted her to.
That's why I went to you! Because she didn't want you
anymore, so I could have you!"

Sarah's parents fell silent. Her brothers looked as if they
were melting into the chairs on which they sat.

"Papa. It wasn't on purpose. She said she was going to
marry Ari. So that meant I could have Yossi."

"But then she changed her mind," I interjected softly.

Sarah nodded. "It wasn't my fault. I wasn't going to tell
her that Yossi was mine until she was married. But then she
changed her mind. She decided not to marry Ari; she decided she loved Yossi. So she went back to Yossi. And
when she was there she saw my sweater and found out

about us. She was so angry. She didn't understand that it wasn't my fault. I only did it because she decided to marry Ari Hirsch. I went to Yossi because she didn't want him anymore. It was my turn. She was supposed to marry Ari Hirsch and that meant I could have Yossi."

"Sarah," I said, "What happened?"

"It wasn't on purpose," the girl repeated. "She found out about Yossi and me. And then he didn't want me anymore. I was so angry. I just slapped her, not hard or anything. But she slipped. She just slipped and fell down the stairs. It was so loud. Such a loud crash. I ran down after her, but it was . . ." Sarah paused and waved her hands in the air, as if she were pushing something away. "It was so messy. Her head was wet and bloody. Her neck was all crooked."

"Did you put her in the freezer?" I asked.

"Yes."

"Why?"

"I had to put her away. It was so messy." Sarah's voice was affectless and flat. "She fit in there just right. Once I had her in I just plugged the freezer in. So she wouldn't get spoiled."

At that her parents, who had been staring silently, erupted in loud, anguished sobs. Nettie stood against the wall, her hand clamped over her mouth, her eyes wide with horror. Yossi crumpled onto the floor, kneeling with his head bowed and his eyes streaming.

I remembered the broken saucer hidden away in a pocket. At the time, I thought that Sarah had so carefully hidden her misdeed because she was afraid of her parents. I assumed that Sima or the rabbi had terrorized her into feeling that she couldn't make a mistake. But now I realized that, like some of the sociopaths whom I'd represented, this deeply disturbed girl was simply unable to respond in anything resembling a normal manner. She hid her broken saucer. She hid her broken sister.

"No," Fraydle's father said suddenly, shaking his head. "This did not happen. Some stranger did this. You!" He pointed at Yossi. "You did this! Not my daughter. No."

Yossi shook his head wordlessly, tears spilling out of his eyes and down his cheeks.

"Rabbi," I said, "the police will figure it out. They'll find evidence, maybe Sarah's fingerprints or something else. You must get a lawyer right now and go to the police. She's a minor; she's clearly disturbed. The lawyer will be able to help you figure out a strategy."

"No!" he shouted again.

"Rabbi, they will never believe that a stranger did this."

"So I will tell them it was me! It was me." He wasn't shouting any longer, but his voice was loud.

"No, Baruch," Sima whispered, through her tears. Her voice grew firmer. "You will not do this. You will not take responsibility for this. We will do what Mrs. Applebaum says. We will find a lawyer to help Sarah."

"But—" he began.

"No," she said.

Twenty-seven

I left Fraydle's family with the lawyer, a Hasid, who had come as soon as the rabbi called. They didn't need me anymore. I left quietly. I stood for a moment on the front steps of the house, looking out at the street where the Finkelsteins' community had gathered. A few men looked at me, and I lowered my eyes. I felt a hand on my arm and turned to find Nettie. She reached an arm around my shoulders and whispered, "Thank you."

"Thank you? For what?" Ruining her life and the lives of her family even more than they'd been ruined before? After all, what good had I done? I hadn't saved Fraydle; she was gone. And because of me their other daughter was lost to them forever.

"Oh, Nettie, you were right. The truth is a terrible thing. I'm so sorry for what I did," I said.

"For what *you* did? You did nothing wrong. What, you

think you had something to do with this? Don't be silly."
She squeezed my shoulder.

"If I hadn't gotten involved, you might never have found
out about Sarah."

"Juliet, with or without you, our darling Fraydle, *aleha
ha shalom*, would still be dead. With or without you, we
would have found her body. And then, with or without you,
Sarah's guilt would have come out. The only thing you did
was spare us months of uncertainty."

I nodded, embarrassed at my own self-centeredness.
Was I really looking to *her* to comfort *me*?

"If you need anything, call me, okay?" I said.

She patted me on the arm. I put my arms around her and
we hugged for a moment. I kissed her on the cheek and
walked down the steps and through the crowd, which parted
for me as if I were Moses and they the Red Sea.

When I pulled into the driveway of my house, I sat for a
moment in my car, thinking about the Finkelsteins. They
would not need to bear this tragedy alone. I knew that moments from now Sima's kitchen door would open and
women would begin to stream through, their arms laden
with casseroles of *tsimmes* and thick soups of chicken and
barley. They would pile the *babkas* and the sponge cakes
on the counters and prepare the first of endless cups of tea.
The low murmur of their voices would fill the room and the
air would be redolent with the smell of talcum powder and
food and the warmth of women. Their husbands would
pour into the living room like a sea of dark coats and hats.
Some would rock back and forth in prayer. Others would
simply stand in the corners of the room, talking in soft,
deep voices. Or perhaps they would be quiet—not sure
what to say to a family burdened with such incalculable
pain. The Finkelsteins' house would fill to bursting with

the members of their community. The compassion and support of the men in their long beards and dark clothes and of the women with wigs so carefully covering their shorn heads would give to Sima and Baruch the strength they needed to get through the horrible and harrowing weeks, months, and years ahead.

Suddenly, I thought of my own family. Those three people I loved most in the world. I wanted to be with them, to be surrounded by them. *They* were my community. Peter, Ruby, and Isaac were my universe. I got out of the car and walked up the stairs to my apartment. I could hear Ruby's bubbling laugh. I started to run, desperate to see them and to be back in the center of my own little world. I burst through the back door and found them sitting around the kitchen table. Peter held Isaac in his lap and Ruby sat across from them, a pile of chocolate chip cookies in front of her and her face painted with a milk mustache.

"Mama!" she shouted, when she saw me. I leaned over and kissed her milky, chocolatey face.

"Hi, sweet girl."

Peter reached out with his free arm and grabbed me around the waist. He squeezed me to him and I leaned on his warm, strong shoulder.

"Tell me," he said.